A
DOZEN
Short Ones

A DOZEN
Short Ones

Timothy Benson

A DOZEN SHORT ONES

iUniverse books may be ordered through booksellers or by contacting:

iUniverse
1663 Liberty Drive
Bloomington, IN 47403
www.iuniverse.com
844-349-9409

Because of the dynamic nature of the Internet, any web addresses or links contained in this book may have changed since publication and may no longer be valid. The views expressed in this work are solely those of the author and do not necessarily reflect the views of the publisher, and the publisher hereby disclaims any responsibility for them.

Any people depicted in stock imagery provided by Getty Images are models, and such images are being used for illustrative purposes only. Certain stock imagery © Getty Images.

ISBN: 978-1-6632-1931-2 (sc)
ISBN: 978-1-6632-1930-5 (e)

Library of Congress Control Number: 2021904354

Print information available on the last page.

iUniverse rev. date: 03/12/2021

Rumor Has It

The Trailside Diner looked like so many small, nondescript cafes that dotted the highways all over the country; white clapboard siding, a green shingle roof and a tired old neon sign that was barely bright enough to read. Mark was only a few steps inside the entrance when a sturdily built woman with a black apron wrapped around her ample hips walked up to him. "Mornin', hon, you can sit anywhere you'd like."

"I'm meeting someone here", he replied, just as a man in a Stetson hat, waving at him, caught his attention. "Oh, I think that's him there in the first booth." He smiled at her, walked toward the man and asked, "John?"

"That's me." The man smiled and stood up, extending his hand. "John Meecum, and Mark, I recognize you from your picture in your weekly column." *What You Should Know*" by Mark Driscoll is on my regular reading list."

They shook hands and sat down. "Gee, I've only been with the paper for six months and you're the first person who's recognized me. Is that enough to make me a celebrity?" He laid his laptop case on the booth seat beside him.

Before they could settle into their seats the woman in the apron came over and stood by the table. The red plastic name tag on her blouse told them her name was Dorie.

"Can I get you boys some coffee to start?"

John answered, "Sure, mine's decaf and black."

Mark added, "Mine's regular."

Dorie nodded and sighed. "Two men, two pots…okay." She walked away shaking her head.

John watched her for a moment, smiling, then said, "I get the impression she thinks we're overworking her."

While Mark opened his bag and pulled out a few things he said, "I appreciate your meeting me here this morning, John, especially because this place isn't exactly on the beaten path. And unless you have an objection I'd like to record our conversation."

John waited while Mark laid a small recorder on the table and turned it on, then replied, "Oh, I'm glad to do it. From what you told me on the phone it sounds like you're working on an interesting story."

"Well, I hope it will be, and having a local historian like you help me fill in some background stuff really helps."

Mark unfolded a small map and laid it on the table between them. The title block read *PLANNED ELK CREEK ESTATES*. Before he could begin his presentation to John, Dorie returned carrying a tray. She set the two coffee pots on the table then cups in front of each of them. "You boys hungry this mornin'?"

Mark looked at John and seemed to read his mind. "We'll need a few minutes to look at the menu first, if you wouldn't mind coming back in a little while."

Again she sighed. "Sure, no rush." As she turned to leave she looked down at the map and saw the title. "Oh, that's the big, new housin' project up on Elk Creek Road. I hear it's really gonna' be first class."

Even though the project wasn't a secret Mark didn't want a lot of people to know he was involved in any way, especially the fact he was writing an article about the developer. "Yep, that's the one." He reached for his pot of coffee and filled his cup, his arms and hands purposely blocking her view of the map. She looked at both men and walked away.

John was smiling. "I hope you didn't think Elk Creek Estates was a big secret around here."

"No, but my article is going to be more about Compass Development than the houses and details. They have sort of a reputation and it's not a good one. They're like the Walmart of developers. They come into a town, bring their own people to do the work and screw over the locals."

"John chuckled. "I like your Walmart analogy." He pulled the map toward himself and said, "So tell me what you have here."

"It's a topographical map of the project. The lines that are closer together are the hills and elevation changes on the site. The part here where the lines are farther apart is the flat area in the center where a trailer park is located now. What can you tell me about that?"

"There's not much to tell. The trailers have been there since way back in the early 1970s. The land was part of the old Jacobsen ranch. The story is that when Lars Jacobsen got himself into a little jam with a local girl he needed to buy his way out. He sold that parcel to a trailer park developer. The whole thing happened very quickly and quietly, and the road and trailers were in place in a matter of a few months."

Mark was glad that John was a source for his article. His familiarity with the people and the gossip would humanize the story. "That's interesting. I dug through some filings at the courthouse but didn't find anything about this particular parcel of land, at least nothing unusual."

"That's how Jacobsen operated; quietly, with minimal or no paperwork and cash only. You're new to this town, Mark. Casper is cowboy country and things get done differently here". He turned and looked across the room. "See those two old boys over at the far corner table?

Mark looked at the two grizzled men in jeans and cowboy hats. "Yeah, they look like they've spent their lives on horseback."

John smiled. "Well, they might look rustic to you but don't underestimate them. If you ever do business with them they'll probably end up taking you to school."

Mark laughed, thinking again how much of a journey he'd made from Los Angeles to Casper. "Well, there's something I found out, or I should say, something I heard. At the courthouse the clerk helping me in the file room told me there was a rumor that the trailer park was sitting on an old Indian burial ground. Apparently it was never investigated or proven."

"I've heard that rumor too but nobody really knows for sure, at least not yet. The park went in a couple of years before the American Indian Movement came into being so there was no real activism like there is today. A few local Northern Cheyenne leaders tried to look into it but there was no organized effort so it all died quietly. Then came the trailers."

"So there was no burial ground?"

"That wasn't officially determined. But to make sure nothing stopped him, the developer came up with a bizarre argument for why it shouldn't matter either way. He said the park would only have one trench from the road for water and electrical lines. And since the trailers had no basements and were just set on concrete slabs there would be no disturbing of any services underground."

Mark shook his head in disbelief. "And the city council actually bought that line of shit?"

"Yep, and the tribe never did get its act together. They had some meetings but nothing ever got done and eventually the whole investigation was abandoned. Like I said, this is cowboy country and the cowboys always beat the Indians. But, saying that now, things might change."

"What do you mean?"

John leaned forward, his eyes glancing around the dining room. "I mean when Compass first announced this luxury project, most people thought it was a good thing. An old trailer park eyesore would go away and be replaced with new, modern housing. It sounded like a win-win for everyone, for everyone except the Northern Cheyenne."

"So is the tribe going to try and block this one?"

"Yep, with everything they've got. A few days ago I got a call from Daniel Littlewolf himself, the President of the Northern Cheyenne

Nation. He asked me to help them get some historic background on the area, and I've asked the State Historic Office to look at it too. The governing body of the tribe is the Council of 44 and they have a whole lot of clout at the capitol. I have a feeling this is going to become a lot more than a rumor." He paused, smiled and added, "And this time I think the Indians might finally beat the cowboys."

Marked grinned and asked, "Will it stop the project?"

"At the very least it could delay it by as much as a year, but, depending on what they find, Compass might end up with a bunch of big houses on the hills wrapped around a sacred graveyard, a big piece of ground they can't touch. That's why I think you should work on your story as carefully and quietly as possible. This thing just might get ugly."

They were interrupted by Dorie. "Ready for some breakfast?"

Mark looked at John and shook his head and said, "No, I think I'll just stay with coffee today."

Her frown didn't surprise John and he replied, "Me too, Dorie, just coffee."

She took both pots and refilled their cups. "Excuse me, I don't mean to pry but is that Indian burial ground rumor still goin' around?"

Mark found her meddling both humorous and irritating. Her powers of hearing were amazing. "Well, I'm new around here and I was just curious."

Before she turned to leave she said, "I haven't heard any talk about that in years." They watched her walk across the room to the two cowboys at the front, corner table. "Bud, Howie, you boys doin' okay here? Need anythin' else?"

The men had been deep in conversation and weren't happy about her interruption. The tall, gray-haired man in the corner chair answered firmly, "No, Dorie, I think we're okay, maybe some more coffee in a little while." He waited for her to leave and then turned to his friend. "So, Bud, let me get this straight. From what you're tellin' me we've only got two more signatures to go and then we can call Compass. Who's left on the list?"

"Well, you can probably guess. It's the same two that are always a pain in the ass; Sam Grover and Don Becker."

"Jesus H Christ, what's their problem? We stand to make a killin' when we sell our places but Compass made it clear that it's gotta be all of us or none of us."

"Well, we're close. I think when we tell those two guys that twenty three of us want to sell and they're the only ones draggin' their heels, the pressure will get to em'."

"Did you tell em' what deep pockets Compass has? They'll try to bargain with us on a price but if we do this right we can really jack em' up. Some of us are gettin' ready to retire and all that money will make a sweet little nest egg.

Bud leaned forward and lowered his voice. "Howie, I know what you mean. Our trailers are old and rusted and most of them are like mine, they have a leaky roof and leaky windows. When I went around knockin' on doors I convinced everyone, at least everyone but Sam and Don, that we can get two or three times what the trailers are worth plus a bonus if we move out fast. I also told them if we don't close a deal with Compass real soon there won't be anyone else linin' up to buy their crappy, old mobile homes."

"What do you think it'll take to really convince em'?"

"I don't know. I think maybe if we got Sam out for a few drinks we could get him to come around. He's only on the fence because Mary is attached to the place. It was their first home and where they raised their two brats, but money talks and I think Sam can get her to listen."

"And Don, what's his problem?"

"Oh, you know how he gets. He likes to think he's in charge, the big man of Apple Grove Mobile Park. If it's not his idea then it's automatically wrong. I might need your help with him. In the meantime keep this between the two of us."

Once again Dorie suddenly appeared at their table and started to refill their coffee. She looked at them both and said, "Guys, I'm not pryin' or bein' nosy but did I hear you say the trailer park is sellin' out?"

Bud rolled his eyes and sighed. "Dorie, we're just talkin' here, kind of throwin' out ideas." He hoped she wouldn't show any more interest. She did.

"Like I said, I'm not bein' nosy. It's just that those two guys over there in the front corner are talkin' about the trailer park too and I thought it was kind of a coincidence."

Both men turned and looked over at Mark and John. Bud turned back to Howie. "Recognize em'?"

"Nope, never saw either of em' in here before." They looked at Dorie and she quietly said, "Well, I never saw em' either but they have a funny lookin' map with them. It's the new development, the one with the really big houses, and the one guy said the trailer park was smack in the middle of it."

Howie looked at Mark and John again then back at Dorie. "Do us a favor, let us know if you hear them say anythin' else, okay?" Dorie nodded and walked away.

Howie looked around and said, "I wonder what that's all about. He paused a moment then continued. "Okay, so assumin' we get Sam on board, Don's the only thing standin' in the way of makin' a deal with Compass, am I right?"

"Yep, we get Don to sign on and we're golden. Compass says when we're all on board they'll start writin' checks. Better start thinkin' about what you're gonna do with all that money."

Dorie was back in the kitchen when the two well dressed men walked in. They stood looking around at the four other customers and the four other customers looked right back. The men weren't sure if they should wait or find a seat. Dorie spotted them and called out as she approached them, "Mornin', boys. You can sit anywhere you'd like." She walked over to the waitress station, grabbed a pot of coffee and two menus then followed the men to a booth in the far, back corner. "Geez," she muttered, "I'm walkin' some miles this mornin'."

The men sat in silence while Dorie filled their cups. When she asked them if they wanted to see menus they both said, "Okay." She hovered beside their table for a moment and finally said, "I don't mean to be nosy but you boys don't look like you're from around here." She waited for a reply.

The man in the left seat looked up from his menu long enough to answer, "We're not," then went back to his reading. That was all he said and Dorie took it as a sign they weren't looking for conversation. When she walked away the same man said to his friend, "See, Chad, I told you when you asked to come along, you'd see a lot of local color."

Chad laughed and looked around to make sure no one was within earshot. "That run down old trailer park was a real sight and this place is just as classy. Our project will really help this town get out of its own way."

"Yeah, I can't understand how anyone can live in a place like this. Nothing to do and nowhere to go. Not enough girls and too many trees."

"Mitch, face it, you're the quintessential city boy."

"Yeah, I need my nightlife and a Beemer, not a pick-up truck. I wonder what they do for fun around here."

"Next trip back how about we check out the downtown?"

"Yeah, that should take about fifteen minutes."

They looked over their menus and Mitch waved to catch Dorie's attention. When she reached the table he asked, "Can I get an egg white omelet?"

Dorie seemed surprised. "You mean with just the whites? What about the yolks?"

Mitch sighed. "I want an omelet without the yolks."

"Well then, how is that an omelet?"

He looked over at Chad who was trying to hold back a grin. "Never mind, just give us a few more minutes."

When they saw that Dorie was busily engaged at refilling the napkin holders on other tables they felt comfortable restarting their conversation. Mitch said, "Man, I hope we won't have to make too many more trips to this place."

"Chad nodded in agreement. "I don't think we'll have to. I got a call from some guy from the trailer park on Tuesday and he said they only needed two more signatures and then they could sign off on the property. I got the impression those people think we're going to pay them a fortune for those rusty old boxes. He gave me his number and I told him I'd call him while we're here."

"Good. Unless those damn trailers are gone we won't have a community park and playground in the middle of the place, and without those we won't have a project."

"And without the project you and I might be looking for new jobs."

Neither man had done more than glance at their menus and when Dorie returned she impatiently waited while they did a quick scan of their choices. They both figured it was pointless to ask for anything that wasn't clearly listed on the menu so they both ordered the House Special and told Dorie there was no rush.

They relaxed and talked about the project for a while longer and stopped when Dorie arrived with their orders and more coffee. They sat in silence as she set the plates down.

She looked at them and asked, "Anythin' else I can get you boys?"

Chad answered, "No, we're fine, thank you." He looked up and was curious when she just stood there. "Is there something else?" he asked.

Dorie hesitated for a moment and then said with a heavy sigh, "Boys, I don't mean to pry but I heard you talkin' about the trailer park and it's just so strange."

"What's so strange?"

She turned and nodded toward Mark and John. "See those two boys right there? Well, ever since they first sat down they've been talkin' about the trailer park just like you boys were. And those two old boys there in the corner, they've been here for an hour and all they've been talkin' about is that trailer park." She turned back to Mitch and Chad. "That's what's strange. The six of you are the only people in the whole place and you're all talkin' about the same trailer park."

Mitch and Chad looked at Mark and John, who were looking back at them. Then they looked over at Bud and Howie who were also looking back at them. Then they saw Mark and John looking at

Bud and Howie. Mitch looked nervous when he asked, "Did you hear them talking about anything else?"

Dorie casually started refilling Chad's cup and answered, "No, not much, just that there's an old, sacred Indian burial ground right under those trailers."

Past, Present, Past

Charlie hadn't expected to run into the long stretch of yellow construction tape strung between the trees. There were a few clouds in the sky but there was enough moonlight to see that the tape was wrapped around the entire property. He'd parked his car a block away and it was under a group of trees that hid it from the streetlights. He stood under a large maple tree and scanned the area. He had to find a path to the backdoor of the house that would give him as much cover as possible. It was after midnight and there were no lights on in the two nearby houses. He looked up and down the street and when he was sure there were no cars coming he ducked under the tape, held the box against his chest and half walked, half ran to the house.

The Copley mansion had sat on a hill overlooking the town for as long as Charlie could remember. It had been vacant for about three years and after much discussion the family had agreed to sell it to a developer who planned to tear it down. The County Historical Society had worked closely with the developer and family to identify the items in the house that had historical significance and which had value as architectural salvage. Charlie could see from his vantage point on the back porch that the exterior had already been stripped. There was no lock on the door and he carefully pushed it open. Once he was inside he stepped into the kitchen and turned on the small LED flashlight that would guide him through the interior. He shined the narrow blue-white beam over the floor and across the walls, knowing that he had to get the box in place and then get out fast. He took a deep breath and hurried toward the front of the house.

The locals had said many times that the Copley house looked like something out of a Hitchcock movie: Gothic arched windows, a broad slate roof and a front entrance porch that looked both elegant and intimidating. As he stood in the parlor and looked around, Charlie thought how the inside was even spookier than the outside but he didn't have time to gawk. His plan was to hide the box in what he figured would have been the master bedroom and he knew he wouldn't have much time to do it. Every slow, creaking step up the elegant staircase made him more nervous but at least the narrow beam of light kept him from tripping in the dark.

The demolition contractor had been busy. Most of the doors and casings were gone as were the ceiling light fixtures. It was obvious which bedroom had held Milton and Sarah Copley. The master suite was huge and overlooked what were once beautifully manicured gardens. Another window had a view of the town below. It was easy to picture Sarah standing in front of it, starting her day by looking down on people. The bathroom fixtures were gone and most of the tile stripped but it was still clear that the owners had lived a very luxurious life. Now the task was to hide the box in a place where it was sure to be discovered. It took a few minutes with the flashlight but he finally saw that some floorboards had been removed inside a large closet near a dressing room. He focused the beam on the hole and saw a place where he could slide the box between the floor joists. He had to make sure that part of it would be visible. It was a snug fit and he tore his latex gloves pushing it but he managed to get it in place. He fought an urge to indulge his love of antiques and look around the still magnificent house. The longer he stayed the greater the risk of a neighbor or passing police cruiser seeing him. He hurried back down the stairs, across the parlor and kitchen then out the back door. A car was driving by slowly and he hid behind a contractor dumpster until it passed. It took a few minutes but he got back to his car and drove away, keeping his headlights off for a block before turning them on and heading for home. It was a Friday night and he was glad that he could sleep late in the morning.

It was hard for Charlie to get out of bed on Saturday. He'd spent an almost sleepless night filled with thoughts of his scheme, the box and how it had all come about. Back in February, when he'd first heard that the Copley mansion had been acquired by the Historical Society, the story brought back memories that he'd tried for years to forget. They were painful memories, the kind that people try to bury but come back when something triggers them. The name Copley was Charlie's trigger. The news reports about the mansion included old photographs of Simon and Sarah Copley, their son Arthur Copley and his wife Marion and a television interview with their granddaughter, Sarah Copley Powell. Even after the passage of time she was still beautiful, as beautiful as the day she'd broken Charlie's heart and embarrassed him in front of half the school.

Charlie Matthews was the epitome of average. Average height, average weight, a C-average student. Even his last name put him right in the middle of the classroom seating chart. He wasn't part of the small group at the top who were smart or rich or athletic and he wasn't part of the small group at the bottom who struggled with grades or who had a reputation for getting into trouble. He was part of the large group in the middle who never got much attention from the people outside it. That made him one of the last people who should have had a romantic interest in Sarah Copley. She was the prettiest girl in the school, well dressed, straight A's and a member of everything from the Student Council to the Drama Club. She was unattainable but Charlie was too smitten with her to see it. And her television interview had brought back every memory and every detail of that April day in his senior year, that day when he'd nervously approached her in the school cafeteria and asked, "Excuse me, Sarah, but I was wondering if you'd go with me to the Spring Dance."

Everyone has heard the old expression, "If looks could kill" and Charlie was almost killed that day. Sarah had looked at him, first as if she was struggling to recognize him and then as if he was something stuck to the bottom of her shoe. When she'd said to him, "Oh, wow, you've got to be kidding", with a dozen people watching and laughing, he was hurt and humiliated. She'd looked at him again and asked, "Are you serious, me go with you?" He'd quickly turned and walked out of the cafeteria, down the hallway and out the back door. He couldn't bring himself to face anyone and walked home. The sting of her words stayed with him for a long time. If he saw her in the hallway he'd turn and walk the other way. He wasn't even sure that she knew his name. He'd decided not to ask another girl to the dance because he didn't want to see Sarah with another guy. It wasn't until after graduation, when he didn't have to see her or be anywhere near her, that his humiliation began to fade and turn into quiet, buried anger.

That Saturday morning while Charlie sipped his coffee in his house full of antiques, he thought back to the day his little scheme had been born. Even though it would come in handy on his project, he knew that his near obsession with collecting antiques and memorabilia had been just one of the things that had made Laura leave him after just four years of marriage. In the divorce he got the mortgage payment and his collection of old things and she got everything else. Once again in his life he was lonely and once again he was angry. The news of the Copley mansion and Sarah's interview had set off something inside him. In just a few days he'd created a plan to balance the scales with Sarah Copley. He'd told himself over and over it would just be a prank but as it developed in his mind he couldn't deny there was a certain kind of darkness to it.

His plan for giving Sarah her comeuppance was based on the fact that she and her entire family had always felt they were some kind of local royalty. Her grandfather owned several large businesses and tracts of prime land all over town. Her grandmother, for whom she'd been named, was a pillar of local society and influential in the local Baptist Church, and her holier-than-though attitude toward people seemed to have been passed down to her granddaughter. That attitude became the basis for Charlie's plan. It would be his own twisted version of a time capsule, a capsule that would give the town a different view of the Copley name.

Hours and hours of online research led to the design of the capsule. He'd focused on the events and attitudes of the mid-1900s when the Copley family had first begun building their little empire. The capsule itself and its contents had to be legitimate products of the era and it turned out that Charlie already had something that would work perfectly; a lidded box made of green Bakelite. Bakelite was the world's first type of plastic, invented in the early 1900s and had become popular for making all kinds of toys and household items. The contents of the green box took longer to select. He knew that time capsules were meant to keep history alive, to give people of the future a glimpse of people in the past. The contents were meant to give the best and most positive view of the time. Charlie's idea was exactly the opposite. His idea was to create a box to burst the Copley bubble.

Slowly over the next few weeks the collection of items began to take shape. The Historical Society had a large cache of old black and white photos and he'd found several shots of Milton and Sarah. To maintain the secrecy of his project he'd used his phone to take close-up pictures of the photographs rather than ask permission to use the Society's photocopier. Online searches turned up photos of people partying in bars and speakeasies. Visits to two of his favorite antique shops provided an old, perfectly intact package of Lucky Strike cigarettes and a small metal whiskey flask. He was even able to find a partial box of old stationery. He had the raw materials for the capsule. Now he had to bring it to life.

As a source of inspiration Charlie took his high school yearbook from the shelf, opened it to young Sarah's photo and laid it on the desk in front of him while he worked on the box. Then he began his little time travel project. The first two items were easy. He poured a very small amount of whiskey into the flask and sealed the cap tightly. He carefully opened the pack of Lucky Strikes and removed half of the cigarettes. Those two items were things that a devout Baptist woman of the era would never have touched, except for Sarah Copley. The third part of the contents took a bit longer. He'd printed out the online photos of life in the bars and speakeasies of the day but they would be meaningless until Sarah showed up in them. After a few hours working in Photoshop he sat back in his chair and looked at the results. There was Sarah Copley, the leader of local high society, wearing a tight, shiny silk dress and hoisting a mug of beer with a group of fellow bar patrons. In another shot she sat demurely at a table, cigarette in hand, smiling for the camera. Sarah Jane Copley, matriarch of the family, was a naughty girl. Charlie printed out the fake images on photo paper and wrinkled and rubbed them enough to give them an aged look.

The last part of the capsule was the one that Charlie had been uncertain about. The other items in the box were more playful than nasty, and for a moment he'd considered just going with what he'd already put together. Then he looked at the yearbook again, at the picture of the pretty girl who had mocked and embarrassed him in front of a crowd. He stared at her expression, more smirk than smile. He heard again her snotty answer to his invitation. And he felt the same sick feeling in the pit of his stomach. Suddenly, his uncertainty faded and he began the last and maybe best part of the time capsule's content.

The old stationery slowly became letters, love letters from a man named John who'd pledged his love to Sarah Copley. The married Sarah Copley. The Bible-toting teetotaler Sarah Copley. Yes, that Sarah Copley. Charlie chose his words carefully, trying to express John's longing for a woman he wasn't sure he could have. There were light moments of fun and laughter. There were confessions of a deep and real passion. And there were pleas for Sarah to leave Milton and escape with John to a life of travel and adventure. The other items in the green box just made a statement but the letters made it a box full of scandal. Small town bubble bursting scandal. Charlie folded them carefully without envelopes and tied them into a bundle with a satin ribbon. It took him a few minutes to arrange everything in the box and it was a snug fit. Before he closed and latched the lid he took out his phone and took a few photos of the contents. Within a few days a new chapter in the Copley family history would begin.

Creating the time capsule had been an emotional time for Charlie, wrestling with old, nearly forgotten pain and new anger that had filled him every day he worked on the project. He'd wondered if there was something mentally wrong with his actions. More than once he'd asked himself if he was being driven by his sense of humor or a desire for some kind of revenge. He hadn't yet reached that answer.

As he finished his last sip of lukewarm coffee on that Saturday morning he knew that the only thing left to do was wait. Wait for that worker prying up the old floorboards to find a green Bakelite box between the joists. Wait for the box to be opened and examined by someone at the Historical Society. And wait to see if fake memories of people from the past would have any effect on people of the present.

It was on Wednesday, while he sat eating his lunch at his desk and looking over the morning paper, that he saw a small article with the headline COPLEY DEMOLITION REVEALS SURPRISE BOX. He stopped and looked around the office as though he was doing something illegal. Under the headline was a photo of old Sarah looking like the epitome of class and propriety. Charlie began reading. The person who wrote the article referred to the capsule as a small box filled with memories of the home's prominent owner, Mrs. Sarah M. Copley. There was no description of the contents except to call them "handwritten letters and other items of a personal nature". Charlie read the paragraph again and thought, "Gee, maybe it won't go any further than this." But when he began the second paragraph he realized that the story would be talked about for some time. The reporter wrote that the box seemed to have been deliberately hidden under the loose floorboards of Mrs. Copley's closet. Charlie smiled when he read that line and he kept smiling when he read that the Director and Chief Curator of the Historical Society were weighing a decision whether or not to release more information. It was clear that they knew they had a historical bombshell on their hands and wanted to handle it with caution. Charlie sat for a moment enjoying a real sense of pride for creating the mystery. The last sentence of the article said that the Director would be meeting on Thursday morning at 10:00 AM with a Copley family representative, Ms. Sarah Copley Powell, to discuss the matter.

That was the moment that hit Charlie the hardest. He had to decide if his little prank was finished, if he'd accomplished what he'd set out to do or if there was one last thing to take care of, the thing that would put a bow on everything. By the time he'd gotten home he had his answer.

As he'd sat in his car in the Historical Society parking lot he scrolled through images on his phone, trying to distract him from his nervousness. Every little movement that he caught from the corner of his eye was like a poke to his stomach. Then, at about five minutes to ten, a silver colored Mercedes pulled into the lot and parked by the entrance. Even with the glare and reflection on the windows he could tell it was Sarah. It was time to put an end to the time capsule project.

He opened his car door and stood beside it, waiting. When he saw Sarah's door open he began walking slowly toward her. She looked distraught and angry. It was obvious that she'd been told about the contents of the box. When he was about ten feet from her she looked at him without expression then closed her car door and turned to walk into the building. Charlie called out, "Excuse me, Sarah, can I ask you a question?"

She turned toward him, glaring. She sighed and answered, "Do I know you? What do you want?"

Charlie stopped a few feet from her and raised his phone screen close to her face. She saw a photo of the scandal, the open green Bakelite box. He smiled and asked, "I was wondering if you'd go with me to the Spring Dance."

Catching Tomorrow

A narrow beam of early spring sunlight found its way through a gap in the window blinds and when Matt rolled over in bed it hit him in the face. He put his hand over his eyes and let out a long sigh. "Well," he thought, "Daylight Savings Time or not, if I have to turn the clock ahead and lose an hour of sleep I'm glad it's on a Sunday." He laid there staring at the ceiling for a few minutes and then reluctantly got out of bed.

He'd been divorced for only a month but already had his new morning routine down pat. It was a small pot of coffee, a quick read of the morning paper on his tablet and half an hour to shower and dress. He'd been trying to learn some simple cooking for the dinner hour but breakfast was usually found at a drive-through window on the way to the office.

His coffee in hand, he stood for a moment looking out the window at his freshly mown lawn. He'd always taken a lot of pride in his yard and gardens, especially in the spring. The neighbors often commented on how perfectly he maintained things. He confessed, only to himself, that it was an obsession. Another minute of taking in the view then he sat down at the counter and opened the paper on his tablet. Before he even saw the headline he read the date in the upper left corner; Tuesday, March 10. "No, it's Sunday," he thought, "what's up with this?" He slid his phone closer and looked at the screen; Tuesday March 10. "This can't be right." he muttered as he stood up and stared again at the two screens. It was only Daylight

Savings Time, one lousy hour ahead," he thought, "how could I have slept for forty-eight hours?" A quick look at the local TV news only confirmed what he'd already feared. Two days had passed.

He hurried into the bedroom and in fifteen minutes he was putting on his last clean shirt from the closet. Five minutes later he threw his laptop bag into the backseat of his car and headed downtown. The heavy freeway traffic was another sign that it wasn't Sunday. The drive-time DJ on the radio confirmed it with the greeting, "Happy Tuesday, everyone!" The closer he got to his office the more confused he became. "What in the hell happened?" he muttered to himself.

As he got off the elevator and headed down the hallway it seemed as though he was being ignored by his coworkers. The usual greetings and waves were missing and it made him both curious and uncomfortable. He was no sooner settled at his desk when his assistant walked in. "Morning, Anne," he said, trying to sound normal.

"Good morning, Matt, and I sure hope it stays that way." She dropped slowly into the chair in front of his desk. "Mind telling me why you didn't return any of my calls and e-mails yesterday? Everybody was wondering where you were. McClain is really pissed. The CynTech account is his biggest priority around here."

Matt hesitated, trying to get his bearings. "Yeah well I uh, I wasn't feeling well and I stayed in bed all day." He didn't like lying to her but it was all he could think of on the spur of the moment.

And you couldn't at least call me and tell me?" Before Matt could answer she added, "Never mind, let's just try to pull things together. We only have until tomorrow at two. Laurie and Dave are waiting for your direction and I'll need everything from you by nine tomorrow morning to put the Power Point and Zoom agenda together." She leaned back in the chair and looked at him without expression.

The strangeness of his situation still swirled in his head. He waited a moment and then replied, "Thanks, Anne, and don't worry, even if I have to finish things at home tonight I'll get it done."

The rest of the day was full of tension and pressure. Matt's mind was constantly switching back and forth between the presentation and his lost two days. He worked until six and then packed up his files and laptop. The Tuesday rush hour traffic was starting to thin out and he pulled into his driveway earlier than he expected. Dinner was a reheated piece of leftover lasagna, his first attempt at post-marriage cooking. For the rest of the evening he dug through his notes and struggled to focus on the project. It was nearly midnight when he sat back in his chair and stared at his laptop screen. The presentation looked clear and strong. Anne would add the graphics in the morning and they'd be ready to make their pitch to CynTech. He rewarded himself with an extra-large pour of his usual bourbon nightcap. He laid in bed, his thoughts returning to his two lost day mystery but when the bourbon finally kicked in those thoughts faded away.

He was already sitting on the edge of the bed when the alarm went off at six. He'd awakened around five and couldn't get back to sleep. Worry about his presentation had made getting a good night's sleep impossible. He took his phone and tablet from their chargers and walked into the kitchen. It was important that he got into the office early so he'd decided against making coffee. There was just enough time to sit at the counter for a quick scan of the newspaper. When it came up on the screen he gasped audibly. The date said it was Monday March 26. He was shaking as he grabbed his phone for verification. It read Monday March 26. Whatever confusion and worry he'd experienced from his lost two days suddenly seemed like nothing. He had gone to sleep and when he'd awakened it was six days later.

He sat there, frozen in place, unable to move or process what was happening. If the dates were right on his pad and phone there could only be hell to pay at the office. It meant that he'd missed the presentation and probably lost a potential client. His shower and dressing routine happened in a fog. Was there something wrong with his health or was he was losing his mind? All kinds of strange questions popped into his head as he finished getting dressed. If he'd been asleep for six days why hadn't he peed in his bed? And why wasn't he hungry from not eating for so long? And having just shaved the day before, why had there been only the normal, daily stubble and not almost a week's worth of beard? None of it made sense and he felt totally powerless to change anything.

The morning commute took about as long as it usually did but it seemed like hours to him. Twice he'd considered turning around and driving home in an attempt to postpone the inevitable blow-up at the office but he kept on course and finally pulled into the parking garage. The elevator was crowded and he avoided making any eye contact on the ride up to his floor. The walk down the corridor brought the same chilly indifference from his colleagues that he'd experienced the day before. And was it really just the day before? There was no doubt in his mind that he'd broken the world's record for work-related screw-ups.

It felt like a gut punch when he walked into his office. A large cardboard box sat on his desk, full of his personal items and everything that said the office had once been his. Even the framed photographs of his fishing trip to the Caribbean had been taken down from the wall and placed into the box. He laid his laptop bag on the desk and collapsed into his chair. He felt sick to his stomach. Before he could fully grasp what was going on, Anne walked in. He tried to read her expression and decided it was a mix of anger and sadness. "Morning." was all he could get out.

"Matt, I couldn't be sorrier about this but you gave Mr. McClain no other choice. Your little disappearance from the planet cost us any chance to get the CynTech account. You were missing in action for six days. You let down your team and the company."

Matt straightened up in his chair. "I wish I could explain this to you. Something is going on that I don't understand. It's like time is different for me than everyone else."

Anne stood there frowning and shaking her head. "What's that supposed to mean? Are you okay? Some people are wondering if you've got a drinking problem or something. They say you're the one that always wants them to join you at happy hour, that you're the life of the party."

"It's nothing like that, I don't really drink that much. It's just that I'm confused about the way things are happening around me, about how time is passing. I don't know what else to say."

Anne sighed and said, "Well I don't think Mr. McClain is going to understand that any more than I do. He wanted to talk to you but since we didn't know if or when you'd ever step foot in the office again he scheduled a trip to Seattle." She saw Matt look over her shoulder and when she turned around a very large building security guard was standing in the doorway.

"I'm supposed to escort someone to the front door," he said gruffly, looking right at Matt. "Would that be you?"

Anne started to tear up and said in a shaky voice, "Matt, I am so, so sorry about this."

Matt walked back down the corridor, his laptop bag over his shoulder, the box in his arms and the security guard a few steps behind him. The coworkers who had ignored him on his last two walks down the hall were now staring and whispering. It was as though he was doing a long, slow perp walk in a movie. The corridor seemed a mile long.

When he'd pulled into his driveway he didn't even remember making the trip from the office. Before the garage door closed he looked out and saw that his lawn looked like it hadn't been mowed in weeks. That was the least of the problems that filled his mind as he walked into the house. It was only nine-forty-five in the morning but he poured himself a small and totally inappropriate glass of bourbon and dropped to the sofa.

He took a long, slow sip and closed his eyes, struggling to put his thoughts together in a way that could make any sense of what was going on. When he was home it seemed that everything was normal. Time passed at the usual pace. He felt okay physically. There was no sign of a problem or that anything was different or out of place. But now every night when he went to sleep he woke up to what he thought was the next day but was really days into the future. After an hour of confusing and unsuccessful analysis along with a second glass of bourbon he'd come to the conclusion that he'd lost his mind. It wasn't a conclusion based on science or fact, but it was all he could come up with. It was pure emotion. He didn't bother to finish his bourbon. He set the glass down on the table and laid down on the sofa. By eleven o'clock he was sound asleep.

He didn't remember getting into his bed but the sound of garbage trucks on the street out front woke him up at seven-fifteen the next morning. He knew it wasn't the right day for the garbage pickup but after all that had been happening to him he wasn't really surprised. He saw himself in the hallway mirror as he headed to the bathroom, still wearing his slacks and shirt from the day before. "Or was it really from the day before?" he wondered. He went into the kitchen and as much as he didn't want to know he picked up his tablet and clicked on the morning paper. The dateline read April 28, more than a month from when he'd fallen asleep. He moaned and put his hands over his face trying to hold back tears. "My god," he thought, "is this my new life?"

He went through the day in a haze. He was unemployed and a look at his online bank account showed that a small severance check had been direct-deposited to his account the day after he'd been fired. To him that was today and the deposit hadn't yet happened. His April mortgage and car payments had been deducted. Outside of his house the world seemed to be turning at its normal pace. Inside his house everything seemed to be happening the way it always had. But the two timelines were frighteningly out of synch.

Matt's life settled into a bizarre routine of constantly trying to catch up. Every day he'd awaken to a date that was further and further away. His mailbox filled up every afternoon and the mailman had left handwritten notes for him to bring his mail in daily because the box was too full to fit any more. His beautiful lawn had to be mowed every day in response to multiple notices of violation from the HOA that his property had become an eyesore. Trying to watch his beloved Padres on television was pointless because the entire baseball season had happened in what had been just a few days to Matt. Football season had begun. He couldn't call a friend to schedule a get together to watch a game at his favorite bar because he knew their gathering would end up being on two different days. He felt totally isolated.

His attempts to find a job online had been pointless because any replies to his search arrived weeks into the future, not the day after he'd sent them. The worst part of his ordeal was that bill collectors were hounding him for payment on his house and car. Two of his credit cards had been cancelled after what had felt to Matt like just a few weeks since the last payment. His trips to the grocery store had to be pared back because of his dwindling bank accounts. Being penniless seemed inevitable and there was no way to predict the day when it would happen.

A few days into his entrapment an idea had come to him and he'd wondered if he could break the cycle that had torn his life apart. He'd tried a couple of times to stay up all night, thinking that staying awake would bring time back to its normal movement. All he got for the effort was exhaustion. It was the first time in his life he'd felt totally helpless and so disconnected from anything normal. But he couldn't allow himself to give up his struggle to regain his life.

Almost in a masochistic way he had tracked the time, counting each of his days and comparing them to the dates that came up each morning on his phone and laptop. It was a maddening exercise that he couldn't resist. After a few weeks, his weeks, he'd decided it was borderline self-destructive and he'd stopped. There was nothing to do but try to through each day one at a time. No looking at dates, just the day of the week. It was the only way he could hang on to what was left of his sanity. He'd made that decision one Friday night and awakened on Saturday feeling only a little better.

Just like way back when he was working, Saturdays had always lifted his spirits. Now that he was single again his recreational options had expanded but he couldn't ignore the life maintenance that everyone had. After an arduous turn mowing the lawn that was always overgrown and pulling long-dead vegetables from his garden he showered and sat on the sofa. He remembered Saturdays with his friends; friends that had drifted away because they lived in a different time. His television had become his only constant companion. Whenever he turned it on it was always today.

It was hard to figure which college football game to watch but he'd chosen one simply because there was a commercial playing and he could avoid making a decision. That was enough time to use the bathroom and open a beer. He settled in and by three beers and a whole game later he picked up the remote control hoping to find something more stimulating.

He found a local news station with a very attractive weather girl talking about what was coming. He didn't pay much attention because he knew when he woke up the next day her forecast would be weeks or months old. A commercial allowed him enough time to use the bathroom and when he walked back into the living room he heard her enthusiastic pronouncement: "And remember everyone, tonight Daylight Savings Time ends so make sure you turn those clocks BACK an hour."

The Empty Chair

It was an invitation that I had ignored every five years when it came in the mail; the request for me to go back home for a reunion with my classmates from Greenville High School. It was an ongoing chance to revisit my youth but I'd always given it a pass. Every time I'd opened past envelopes addressed to Ronald Wayne Hastings, which no one ever called me, I simply checked the RSVP box that read "Sorry, I will not be attending", added the words "And my name is Ronnie" and sent it back. Every time I'd checked that box I did it with mixed emotions. Except for a few Facebook and Instagram friendships I'd lost touch with some people I was really eager to see again.

Growing up the way I had wasn't the same way as the other kids. My mother was a loving, hard working woman who'd somehow managed to give me a good life, or at least the best one she could afford. Even during times when she was working two jobs she still had time for me. Being a kid is hard enough at any age and the high school years are the hardest even under the best of circumstances. But I had never lived one day under the best of circumstances because of one thing; I'd never had a father.

Of course there was a man in the equation somewhere but my mother had never told me who it was. Whenever I'd asked her about my father she'd just sigh and look away with words like, "It was a long time ago and he just wasn't ready for a family" or "He wasn't the marrying kind". Nothing else. No name, no details and no more questions, please. My father was an empty chair at our dinner table. I'd finally reached an age and a point where I just stopped asking. Since my home life had only ever consisted of me and my mother, that passed for a normal life to me. It was a kind of normal that I'd accepted. I was the kid without a dad. I'd taught myself how to not think about it except for those times, every once in a while, when a friend would invite me to dinner and I'd sit around a family table that included a man in one of the chairs. It was always something I'd think about for days afterward no matter how hard I'd tried to forget. And when I'd gotten divorced a few years ago I'd wondered how my empty chair at the table would be seen by my own son.

Somehow the invitation to this class reunion had felt different. It was my twenty-fifth, the one that people say, "If you miss all of the other ones at least make sure you go to the twenty-fifth". While that made the sense of obligation feel stronger than in past years, it wasn't by itself enough to change my mind but still, I'd stalled and ignored answering the RSVP. Then, just a week before the deadline for replying I received a notice that would take me back home after all. My mother had unexpectedly passed away two months before and it was a lot for me to deal with. If she had been ill she'd never said a word about it to me on our regular Sunday afternoon calls and I'd never even said goodbye to her. There was a brief trip back for her very simple funeral and I had taken care of as many of the details of her meager estate as I could do over the phone and on email. But death isn't that simple and there were some things that required a signature. I just wanted to wrap the whole thing up once and for all. Since I had to be in town anyway I caved in and checked the "I will attend" box and mailed back the reunion RSVP.

The drive from Charleston to Greenville takes a traveler completely across South Carolina. It's a three hour drive through two hundred years of history, a drive through familiar scenery that I'd made dozens of times over the years. This time the scenery was a blur, lost in the distractions of saying a legal and official goodbye to my mother and the mixed emotions of reconnecting with people from my past. A call on my cellphone was a welcome distraction. "Hey, buddy, what's up?"

"Hi, Dad, are you in your car?"

"Yeah, I left a little early because it's supposed to be rainy up in Greenville."

"I guess that means you're gonna miss my game tomorrow afternoon. Coach just told me I'm gonna be the starting pitcher."

I paused. Having to be away from my son only made my mood worse. "I'm sorry, pal, I wish I would have known you were starting but you know I have to take care of Nana's funeral stuff. I'm the only one that can do it."

"I know, I was just hoping you could get back in time, that's all."

"Ronnie, this is a trip I wasn't planning to take but it's something that I just have to do. I'm going to pop into my class reunion tomorrow night but I'll be back on Sunday and we'll get together for dinner at Hunter's Inn. Call me tomorrow and tell me how the game was, okay?

Even with the road noise I could hear him sigh. "Okay, Dad, I'll call you." Another sigh and "Love you."

"I love you too, buddy."

It was raining when I got into Greenville and I went straight to the lawyer's office. It only took twenty minutes to sign the estate documents and write a check. With the legal part of my task completed the next thing on the list was to finish clearing out the last few things left in Mom's house. The job was easier because I'd already given her furniture and clothes to Goodwill. The only thing left to do was to box up some of her smaller possessions and personal items even though I had no idea what I'd do with them. It was going to be an emotional job.

Every drawer I opened, every box I looked into brought back some kind of memory. Mom had never made enough money to accumulate a lot of jewelry or anything close to being valuable. I'd brought along a couple of corrugated boxes to fill with the things I wanted to keep but after two hours I'd only gathered half a boxful. When I stacked the boxes and items to be discarded by the back door I noticed one white box on the shelf of her bedroom closet. It was well worn, as though it had been handled and opened many times over the years. When I pulled it from the shelf I saw her handwritten label on the lid: *Photographs and Memories* with the words surrounded by a heart.

I carried it to a spot near the picture window then sat down and placed it on the floor between my legs. I ran my hands over the label then slowly pulled off the lid. The contents were a mixture of old photographs, newspaper clippings, letters and even my senior class yearbook. I spent a lot of time flipping through the pages, enjoying pictures of myself on the basketball team, in my role of Homecoming King and my favorite one, my claim to high school fame as a guitarist and singer for a band that we'd named "Rebel Yell". Years of memories take a long time to revisit and by the time I'd separated things into a keep pile and a toss pile it was getting dark. The only thing left in the box was a large manila envelope with the word "Personal" written on the front.

In a strange way I felt like I shouldn't open it. If the contents were important enough for her to keep them separate from everything else and label them "Personal", maybe I'd be invading her posthumous privacy. It took me a moment but I knew I'd regret it if I never knew more about the things that were so important to her. I undid the metal clasp and dumped the contents in front of me. There were letters that I decided not to read, a small book of poems with a dried flower squeezed between the pages, yellowed newspaper stories and photos of me with her over the years. Those photos told my history with her and brought tears to my eyes and a lump to my throat.

The last item in the bottom of the envelope was a small stack of Polaroid photos wrapped in a dried out rubber band that broke when I tried to slide it off. There were ten photos altogether and they appeared to have been taken all in one night. There was Mom in a group of people hanging out at *The Roadhouse* where she tended bar. I'd forgotten how beautiful she was when she was young, There were several shots of a group of seven men, all young, with long-hair and a few with black, brimmed hats. They somehow looked familiar but I couldn't make any kind of connection. The last two photos showed Mom with one of the guys. In the first one he was standing behind her with his arms around her waist. She had labeled it "Ronnie and Me". In the second one she was sitting on the same man's lap with a smile bigger than I'd ever seen on her face. On the back of the photo was written "Crazy about Ronnie". Besides noticing my mother's big smile I'd also noticed something that gave me a chill. The man in the photos, Ronnie, looked just like me; the same hair and eyes, even the smile. He was a slightly younger version of me.

It was hard not to stare at the photos as I sorted through the stack three more times. On the margin of each one was the date 10-19-77. It didn't mean anything to me except that it would have been a week before Mom's twenty-second birthday. My curiosity was growing and it was getting late. I put everything back into the envelope, tossed it into the box of items I wanted to keep and then carried everything out to my car. There were two boxes of things I'd planned to get rid of but I knew I'd be digging through them at least one more time before I'd part with anything else.

Back in my hotel room I pulled a small flask of rye whisky from my overnight bag and sat down on the bed, the manila envelope beside me. I spread the contents out with a plan to study them more carefully, beginning with a closer look at the Polaroids. My resemblance to the man named Ronnie was interesting and unsettling. I kept the photos in front of me and began digging through the rest of the contents. When I unfolded a page from an old issue of the Greenville News I was startled by the photos. The paper was dated October 21st, 1977 and the entire front page reported the crash of a plane carrying the rock band Lynyrd Skynyrd. Two photos of the crash scene were accompanied by a larger picture of the band. I froze when I saw it. The man in the middle of the group was Mom's friend, Ronnie. The story said the crash had happened the day before on a flight from Greeneville to Baton Rouge, Louisiana. Three people had been killed including lead singer and guitarist Ronnie Van Zant. Another page was from the *Jacksonville Daily Record* and showed the obituaries for the three local band members, including Ronald Wayne Van Zant.

The whole thing really hit me hard and I leaned back against the headboard, trying to grasp everything I'd just seen. Some quick math in my head told me that my birthday, July 12th, 1978, was roughly nine months after the crash, or more importantly, after the party at *The Roadhouse*. My full name, the timing of my birth and the physical resemblance could only mean one thing: I was the illegitimate son of a rock and roll legend.

There were so many questions that I knew would never be answered. Why had my mother kept it a secret for all those years? Why hadn't she ever told me? Was it an embarrassing youthful indiscretion or a romance? Was she ashamed? Did anyone else know the truth? Was she going to tell me before she died? Would I have been better off not knowing? One thing I knew for certain was that my father's legacy was his music not a son in South Carolina that he didn't know anything about. My own legacy was a work in progress and it wouldn't include him.

I couldn't help but wonder what had gone through my mother's mind every time she looked at the empty chair at our table. I sat there, my flask in one hand and the photos of them together in the other. It was hard to know how to feel or what to do next but, on an impulse, I lifted my flask, touched it to the photo and said, "Mom and Dad, here's to you."

Saturday included a long drive around town looking at the places where my youth had played out; my elementary school, the grocery store where I'd gotten my first job and the other grocery store where I'd worked after I'd been fired from the first one. I sat in the parking lot of my high school reliving the good times and bad times that I knew would be remembered aloud at the reunion, more than likely exaggerated and altered with time. After a long phone conversation with my son about his winning performance I ate a small dinner in the hotel café and then headed to the festivities.

Maybe I should have attended a previous reunion so the shock wouldn't have been so great. Struggling to recognize friends and classmates that you hadn't seen in twenty-five years is almost painful. Some people age better than others but they still age and twenty-five years is a quarter of a century. The jocks had gained a lot of weight and the cheerleaders had had a lot of work done. Thankfully, the nametags they gave out were large enough to read at a discrete distance, before I'd have to exchange any greetings.

The first half hour was spent at the cash bar where I enjoyed drinking a reasonably good Scotch and playing "Who the hell is that?" as people walked by. In the process I'd reconnected with a few friends who shared with me a promise to find each other on Facebook. I wondered how many of them would actually follow through. I'd just ordered another Scotch and was prepared to wade into the crowd when a voice behind me called out, "Hey, Ronnie, my man!"

I turned and, without even looking at his nametag, recognized an old friend and bandmate. "Hey, Scott!" His red hair had turned mostly gray but his toothy grin and freckles gave him away.

"I'm good. When I heard you were finally coming to one of these I told my wife, 'I'll believe it when I see him.'"

"Well, they say everyone should go their twenty-fifth so here I am." I noticed he was holding an empty glass and asked, "What are you drinking, it's on me?"

"Well, I've graduated from beer like we did back in the day to whatever Scotch is on hand."

"Me too." I hoisted my glass to the bartender and pointed to Todd. A moment later we were drinking together for the first time in twenty-five years. Even though thoughts of my Mom and my newly discovered father never left my mind I'd definitely started to relax. I looked around and noticed everyone was milling around the quiet ballroom. There wasn't the music and dancing I'd expected and I said to Todd, "Man, it sure is dull in here. I thought the invitation said there'd be a band."

Todd smiled. "There is, but we're on a break."

"You mean you're still playing? I've wondered what happened to all you guys after we broke up Rebel Yell."

"Well, after graduation when you left for college Dean, Marty and I all kind of went our separate ways for a while but we all stayed in town. We got together at the tenth reunion and decided to put a new band together. We're The Locals, kind of a mix of Country,

Americana and Roots Rock. We even do some of the same stuff we did when you were with us."

It was like an omen of something that was meant to happen. I threw back the little bit of Scotch that was left in my glass. "Do you still play with an extra guitar like you used to?"

"Oh yeah, we all like to mix things up, why?"

I hesitated, thinking about everything that had happened in the last forty-eight hours. "Well, I'm pretty rusty but if you guys wouldn't mind I'd like to get up there and play something with you."

Todd sounded excited. "Hell yeah, what do you want to play?"

I smiled and answered, "How about *Free Bird*"?

Home Again

Nothing about a cross-country move is easy. The amount of work and upheaval to a person's life seem to almost outweigh the reasons for moving in the first place. Almost.

The dashboard clock read 9:32 AM but Zack could already feel the sun through his open car window. The Arizona summer heat lasted until mid-October but he and Sarah had decided that hot summers were better than cold winters. Their decision to leave Michigan and move to the southwest was a long time in the making, something they'd talked about for years but could never seem to take the big step. But both of their careers seemed to be stalled, most of their families had already moved on to other parts of the country and now seemed like the perfect time for them to do the same. In July they'd done online searches for job possibilities and then in August they'd taken some of their vacation time and flown to Phoenix to interview. They'd figured on a long, slow process but were surprised when they both quickly found jobs. They couldn't wait to get started on the next chapter of their life. Zack had driven out ahead of their final move to begin some training and orientation. Sarah had stayed back in Michigan to sell the house and coordinate things with the moving company. Despite the chaos they looked forward to the adventure of it all.

At 9:45 he got a text message from the realtor he'd been waiting for. It read: "Zack, sorry, stuck in traffic on 101. Should be there in ten. Bob." Zack leaned back in the driver seat and let out a long sigh.

He and Sarah were excited about their new home, a contemporary Spanish-style at the end of a cul-de-sac. It sat on a large lot and the lots on either side hadn't yet been developed so neighbors were a comfortable distance away. It seemed odd to him that the two empty lots had utilities run from the street but no one had ever built on them. Their realtor, Bob Avery, had told them their house had been on the market for over a year which was surprising given its immaculate condition and beautiful setting. When they'd asked him why it hadn't sold he'd gotten tongue tied and said, "Oh, every house has its own time on the market." It was a vague and not very satisfying answer. But the home inspector's report was very thorough and said everything was in good condition and as Zack sat in the driveway looking at their future home he couldn't help but feel excited.

He got out of his car and made a slow walk around the outside of the house. The entire property was landscaped with native cactus, yucca and agave. Two spreading mesquite trees shaded the patio. The watering system had been upgraded and Zack figured his days of long, tedious yard maintenance were over. By the time he got back to the driveway Avery had arrived.

"Sorry, Zack," he said as he got out of the car. "The eastbound traffic is usually pretty light."

"Well," Zack replied, "My commute will be west in the morning and east in the evening so I might have to learn some patience."

Avery handed Zack a brightly colored canvas bag with his company logo on the side. "I brought you the second garage door opener and the extra set of keys that we forgot to get from the Bradshaws before the closing. You said that you sent the other set to Sarah so hang on to these. There are also some chocolate truffles in there and a bottle of Chardonnay for a celebration when she gets here."

"Oh, that's really nice of you. We'll toast you when we finally pull the cork." He turned back toward the house and asked, "Hey, Bob, I don't remember if I asked you this before but do you have any idea what's going on with the lots on either side of us? Do you think we'll have neighbors anytime soon?"

Avery seemed nervous and hesitated as if he was searching for words. "Uh, well, I'm not aware of anything specific right now but you never know"

It was another vague answer that didn't satisfy Zack. "I just don't get why they're still vacant.

Avery's nervousness was still obvious. He changed the subject as he opened his car door. "I think that does it. You signed all of the papers and everything's filed so I guess it's your new home sweet home now." He reached toward Zack and as they shook hands, he said, "Better get those truffles and wine into your new fridge. It's getting hot out here."

As he watched Avery head out of the cul-de-sac Zack used the new remote control and opened the garage door, then went into the kitchen and put the bag into the refrigerator. He'd told the people in his new office that he wouldn't be in until late morning so he took a few minutes to walk around the house.

He and Sarah had fallen in love with the place from the first moment they'd walked in. Saltillo tile floors throughout the living space, hardwood floors in the bedrooms and daylight filling every corner. The original owners, Hank and Lily Bradshaw, an older couple, had meticulously maintained every part of the place, inside and out. It was as though no one had ever lived there. Zack's favorite feature was the large archway between the entry foyer and the living room. It was a high, curving arc of white stucco brightly painted with a traditional Mexican flower and vine motif. It was the focal point of the entire floorplan. He'd been through the house a half dozen times and every time he'd stop, look up at the archway and run his hands over the band of vines. It was really special to him.

His workday was the typical orientation; a mix of meeting new people and learning more about his job duties. In the afternoon he called Sarah. It rang four times at the other end before she answered breathlessly. "Hi, honey. I was just packing the next to last box. I think we're almost ready for the mover."

"That's great, babe. I wish I was there to help you out but the situation is what it is."

"Don't worry about it. Dave and Lynn have been over to help out and a guy from the mover brought some boxes and stayed around to help me with them. The truck comes on Friday morning and I think it'll go just fine. Did you get your travel plans worked out? What time does your flight leave?"

"Everything's set. My flight leaves at 10:20 and I should get in there about 3:30 your time. Do you remember where to pick me up?"

"Yeah, I'll wait in the cellphone lot and when I see that your flight's on the ground I'll head to the arrival curb. And remember to wear your red polo shirt so I can spot you in the crowd."

"Will do. It's going to be three long days in the car heading back but I'm excited. It'll be the next leg of our adventure."

"I'm excited too. I almost can't believe we're finally doing this, pulling up stakes and moving two thousand miles. It'll definitely be an adventure. Keep in touch, honey."

Zack was wall to wall busy the rest of the day and left the office around 5:30. After he'd gotten back to his hotel he changed clothes and headed to the house. He was curious about how it looked at night. On the way he picked up a takeout dinner at McDonalds and it was almost finished when he pulled into the driveway. It was dusk and the outside lights were on. He remembered Avery telling him they were on a light-sensitive control. He left his car in the driveway and went to the front door to make sure the new key worked. When he clicked on the ornate ceiling light in the foyer he got his first glimpse of the house in something other than brilliant sunshine. It was just as beautiful in the fading light.

He'd just stepped through the archway when he felt an odd rush of wind blow over him. He looked back into the foyer wondering if a window had been left open somewhere. When he turned back to the living room he halted after the first step, not sure of what was happening. His previously empty house was now completely furnished with someone else's furniture. There were even paintings and family pictures on the walls. When he saw the picture over the fireplace he felt a chill. It was a formal looking painting of Hank and Lily Bradshaw.

"What the hell?" he muttered. "What's going on?" He felt a mix of shock and anger and stood there a moment before taking several cautious steps into the living room. Everything he saw said the house was still occupied. It was almost overwhelming. He reached into his pocket, his hands shaking, and took out his phone. "Bob Avery damn well better know what this was all about," he thought to himself. The phone rang five times before going to voicemail. "Bob, it's Zack Marshall. I'm at the house and it's full of the Bradshaw's stuff. What the hell is going on here? Call me back like right now!"

There was too much going through his mind to just sit and wait for Bob's reply. He took a long, deep breath and slowly walked further into the house. He noticed the scent of some kind of flowery candle or air freshener. When he reached the dining room he saw that the table had been set for two people. The sound of muffled voices from the kitchen stopped him dead in his tracks. He listened for a moment. It was a man and a woman talking but he couldn't make out what they were saying. Like it or not he knew he had to go into that kitchen. As he walked to the doorway he felt his anger growing with every step, along with a real dose of nervousness. He was flat out dumbfounded when he saw Hank and Lily Bradshaw standing at the counter.

He struggled to maintain his composure. "Mr. Bradshaw, Hank, what is all this? Why are you still here and what's with all the furniture?" There was no response and not the slightest indication they even knew Zack was in the room. He waited and watched them for a moment and then said in a loud voice, "You aren't supposed to be here. It's my house now!" Again there was no response. Part of him wanted to grab the man and shake him but he decided to take a less aggressive tack and just waved his hand in Bradshaw's face. The man didn't even blink as he picked up a plate of bread and carried it into the dining room. Lily moved to the breakfast bar, directly facing Zack, as she filled two bowls with salad. "Lily, why are you here?" She was no more responsive than her husband. It was as if Zack wasn't even there.

The whole situation seemed surreal and Zack didn't know what to say or do next. His ringing phone decided for him. He pulled it from his pocket and hurried back into the foyer. He'd felt the rush of wind again as he passed under the archway, then looked back and stopped in his tracks. The living room and dining room were empty again; no furniture, no pictures and no Bradshaws. Suddenly nothing made sense. He looked at his phone. He'd been prepared to scream at Avery about the former owners moving back in but now he was speechless. Everything seemed to be back to normal again.

His hands were still shaking when he answered. "Uh...hi, Bob. Thanks for calling back."

Avery seemed hesitant. "Zack, I, uh, listened to your message...a couple times. What's going on?"

Zack couldn't decide what to say, whether to tell him everything that he had seen or just pretend that it never happened. "Bob, I'm not sure what to say. I thought there was a problem but I guess I was wrong."

"You said something about the Bradshaws. Did they leave some of their stuff behind, because if they did I'll call them in the morning to get it cleared out."

"No, uh, I thought they did but after I looked around the place... well, things look okay."

Zack was struck by how long it took for Avery to say anything else and when he finally spoke he sounded evasive. "Well...that's good. You bought yourself a beautiful house at a below-market price and I can't imagine what could be wrong with it. Look, Zack, I have to run now. Best of luck with your new home."

Zack put his phone back into his pocket and looked back toward the empty living room. He couldn't get his head around what he'd just experienced. The house was empty then it wasn't and then it was again. He'd been alone, then he wasn't and then he was again. He retraced his steps in his mind. First he was in the foyer and everything was normal and when he passed under the archway he'd felt a rush of wind blow over him and then the Bradshaws and all of their furniture were there. "And what in hell is that wind?" he wondered. "It's only when I go through the arch and then other times it's not there."

The next morning at his office it he'd tried hard to focus on his work. Every conversation and every meeting happened in a fog. He couldn't avoid thinking about the house and about the people who were there, or who he thought were there. He wondered if his new colleagues thought he wasn't paying attention or that he was some kind of flake. Somehow he'd managed to get through the day and then drove to his hotel. A drink at the bar didn't begin to relax him and neither did sprawling on the bed for an hour. A phone conversation with Sarah happened in a fog and he decided not to tell her what happened at the house, the house that didn't leave any room in his head for thoughts of anything else. As much as he wanted to avoid the same experience he knew he had to go back for another look around.

When he got there he sat in his car for a few minutes, half eager to go into the house and half just as eager to hurry back to the hotel. The outside lights were on again. He took a deep breath, got out of the car and headed to the front door. Inside, the elegant foyer light was bright enough to illuminate the living room, the empty living room. "Okay," he thought, "everything's okay, time to head back to the hotel." But he couldn't convince himself and turned toward the living room. His first step under the archway brought the wind and with his second step the furniture appeared and the lights came on. He closed his eyes in panic but he knew he had to search for an answer to his strange predicament.

Shaking all over, he called out. "Hello, is anyone here?" He walked into the dining room and, like his last visit the table was set, but this time for three people. He turned toward the kitchen and called out, Mr. Bradshaw are you here?" Not surprisingly there was no answer. He knew he had no choice but to enter the kitchen and when he did he'd once again found the Bradshaws.

Sarah had circled the airport four times looking for Zack at both arrival areas. She'd called him on his cellphone and had left a dozen messages but never heard back. It wasn't like him to do something like that. She'd been torn about what to do, stay home and keep trying to reach Zack or head to Arizona. Despite making a dozen more calls to Zack that night, when the moving van pulled up in front of their house the next morning she felt a pressure to follow through with the original plan. It was time to leave. The three day drive had been sheer hell for her; no idea of her husband's whereabouts or what she'd find when she got to their new house. She'd cried almost constantly and found it hard to eat anything. When she'd finally driven up to the curb in front of the house and saw Zack's car in the driveway she was both relieved and angry.

She turned off the car and sat for a moment staring at the house then got out and slowly walked to the front door. She was surprised it was locked. Knowing there would probably be a confrontation with Zack she took a deep breath, unlocked the door and walked into the foyer. Despite her anger she took a moment to glance around and take in the view of their new home. She looked into the living room and thought about the painting she had already selected to hang above the fireplace. She looked at the stucco and ran her hand over the beautiful painted vine The wind that brushed across her as she turned to step through the archway caught her off guard but it was when she saw the furniture that she stopped in her tracks. "What the hell is this?" she thought. She wondered if Zack had bought it all but the style wasn't their taste and it looked well aged. And she knew a large moving truck with everything they owned was just an hour behind her.

The situation was overwhelming and her anger turned to a very real panic. "Zack," she shouted, "are you here?" There was no answer." Zack!" She walked farther and when she saw the dining room with the table set for four, she wondered if she should turn around and leave. She'd felt frozen in place and when she heard unfamiliar voices from the kitchen she felt a chill. She took a few cautious steps toward the kitchen doorway and saw the Bradshaws standing by the open refrigerator. Then she turned and saw Zack sitting at the breakfast bar.

"Zack, what is all this? What's going on?" When Zack didn't answer or even look in her direction she turned to the Bradshaws. "Why are you here? This isn't your house anymore!" There was no response and no acknowledgement that she was standing there.

"Zack, answer me, what the hell is happening?" Zack stood up and said, "Hank, I'm gonna grab a beer, do you want one?"

It had taken a long time and tours of many houses but John and Lynn Billings had finally found their dream house. They both loved the Contemporary Spanish design. They especially loved the graceful arch in the foyer with the hand-painted vines. Bob Avery locked the front door behind him while they waited in the driveway beside his car. Bob was grinning ear to ear as he walked up to them. "You guys are going to love this place. The previous owners kept it in immaculate condition and the end of a cul-de-sac is a really prime location. And those two vacant lots on either side will give you plenty of elbow room. He reached back into his car and took out a brightly colored canvas bag. "Before you leave here are some chocolate truffles and wine for you to celebrate with."

Lynn smiled and took the bag from Avery. John turned and looked back at the house shaking his head. "I still don't understand why this place has been for sale for a year and a half."

Avery smiled. "Oh, every house has its time on the market."

Family

Fully clothed, life size mannequins aren't what you'd expect to see in someone's home. A department store, sure, but not like this. When Maria greeted me at the front door and told me to go on into the living room while she finished a phone call, I didn't think I'd have to compete with plastic people for a place to sit. All I could do was stand there in the middle of the weirdness and wait for her to return. Fortunately that wasn't long and when she walked in I could tell she was a little uneasy.

"Sorry, Luke, I had to wrap up that call. It was important." She noticed I was looking at the mannequins and added, "Oh, well, you saw them. I thought I could move them out before you got here."

I offered a weak smile and glanced over at a male mannequin dressed in full 1940s cowboy regalia, from a big Stetson hat down to fancy black boots, staring straight ahead and sitting in a big leather chair. "That one, that's Uncle Rudy," she said awkwardly.

It was all I could do to keep from laughing at the creepiness but I didn't know her well enough yet and I didn't want to say anything that would offend her. I pointed toward a female mannequin in a fancy red dress and curly black hair. She managed a weak smile. "That's Cousin Anna."

"And him, in the pinstripe suit?"

"That's Cousin Albert, he's Anna's older brother." Before I could think of anything more to say she asked, "Would you mind helping me get them into the guest room?"

44

Moments later I was walking down the hallway awkwardly carrying a fake man as big as I was while Maria carried the woman in the red dress.

I was struggling to stay quiet when all I could think of was asking her, "Why in the hell do you own mannequins and why do they have names?" I knew there was no way I could word it to make it sound like anything but rude so I decided to wait awhile to see if she'd offer up any kind of sensible explanation on her own.

She told me to lay Uncle Rudy on the bed while she gently, almost respectfully, set Anna on to a chair. There was a tone to her voice that told me she was uncomfortable and embarrassed by the situation. When Anna was secure in the chair Maria asked, "Would you mind going back for Albert?" Again I found myself carrying a large, plastic man to the guest room. I laid him down next to the cowboy and stood there for a moment looking at them but trying not to look like I was staring. When that was done we walked back down the hallway to the entry foyer and she said, "Wait here, I'll be right back

I watched her as she walked back down the hallway. She was a beautiful young woman, someone who I wanted to get to know better. She had a kind of artistic, Bohemian style that I found very appealing. A Saturday lunch didn't exactly qualify as a first date but I considered it a normal first step. Her mannequins weren't normal. They were definitely a surprise and it was hard to stand there and not feel the strangeness of it all.

It had only been a month since she'd started working at the ad agency. I was in the creative department and she was in finance so our paths didn't really cross much but when they did there seemed to be a very real chemistry between us. Except for a couple of group lunches we'd never seen each other outside the office. I was hoping this lunch would lead to something more. As she walked down the hallway toward me she apologized again. "I'm sorry for all the delays."

"Don't worry about it, stuff happens," I answered, pretending that everything was normal. We walked outside and got into my car and as we headed to the restaurant there was an uncomfortable silence. I looked over at her and she seemed nervous. I felt like I should initiate some conversation but before I could say anything she looked at me and said, "I know you're probably wondering about them, the mannequins." She hesitated a moment. "They're my family."

Nothing she could possibly have said could have sounded any stranger to me. She was single and lived alone like many young women did but I was certain those other young women didn't share their homes with mannequins with names. And as odd as the situation was, her calling them her family was borderline bizarre. I began to wonder what I'd gotten myself into.

She was looking out the window, wringing her hands in her lap. "Luke, how about we wait until we get to the restaurant and then I'll explain things?"

The place wasn't crowded and we found a table in the back corner of the barroom. Not knowing what kind of story Maria was about to share with me, I was glad for the bit of privacy. We ordered a drink and I was glad to discover she was a beer lover like I was. It was just another little thing for me to like about her. By the time our server had brought our beer and walked away, the tension on Maria's face had become obvious. I think I was as nervous as she was.

She took a sip of beer, paused, then began, "Okay, you must be thinking all kinds of unusual things about me, like I'm crazy or something. I wish you hadn't seen all of that at my apartment but you did and I can't change that." Her voice was shaking. "So here it is." She let out a long breath and began. "I was born in Albuquerque. My parents died in a car accident when I was just two and I was raised by my aunt Grace. She tried to take good care of me for a while but when I was around eight she started acting strange. She was drinking more and more and she was hardly ever home. There were times when she'd be gone for two or three days at a stretch and I'd be totally alone. I had to make my own meals and do my own laundry along with going to school."

I sat there listening and trying to imagine how painful it must have been for her to share a story like that. I reached across the table and held her hand as she continued. "Aunt Grace had a couple of jobs. One was at a department store and some of the things she had to do were to change out the displays and dress and take care of the mannequins. When they got old and worn she talked the manager into letting her have them, or at least that was what she told me, and she brought them home. In her own strange way she thought she was doing something nice and told me they were for me to play with. I guess they sort of became the family I didn't really have."

We were interrupted by our server and it took a few minutes to order food that I didn't think either of us was in the mood to eat. When the server left I squeezed Maria's hand and said, "We don't have to talk about this anymore."

"No, it's okay. Actually, it feels kind of good to finally tell someone." She paused and then continued her story. "The first one Aunt Grace brought home was the woman in the red dress. I named her Anna after a girl in a book I read who was pretty and had lots of friends. About a month later she brought home the cowboy. I named him Uncle Rudy after a man I saw on TV who was always in charge of things and took care of problems. It was about six months later when she brought home Albert. I'd decided that Anna needed a big brother to look after her." She stopped for a moment with a faraway look on her face.

I wanted so much to say or do something that would make her feel better but I couldn't think of anything that would be appropriate for the place and the odd situation.

She continued. "We lived in an old house that was kind of outside of the main neighborhood so the other kids didn't come by my house very often. I was alone a lot and it was awful. So my fake family was all I had to keep me company. It was the same way through high school. When I'd make a friend and she wanted to come to my house I was too embarrassed and made up all kinds of excuses to avoid having anyone see how I lived. Fortunately I had a really nice guidance counselor who tried her best to help me but there wasn't much she could do to make my home life any different. But what she did for me was help me get a scholarship to college and when I left home I was hoping things would be different there. I made a few friends but they lived off campus in nicer places than I could afford.

When holidays came they went home to their real families and I went home to…well, I went home to mine." There was a long pause and I knew she had more to say. "When I came to Phoenix and got my job and my apartment I just couldn't let go of them. I still needed them."

Our order arrived and I was hoping it would be the cue for her to shift gears and think about happier things. Every bite of food and every sip of beer seemed to pull her thoughts from the past to the present. I brought up a few things that were going on at the office and even got her to smile a few times. We each ordered a second beer and things finally felt relaxed.

She looked at me with a sheepish smile. "Luke, I'm sorry that I laid all that stuff on you."

I reached for her hand again. "Don't worry about it. I asked you to lunch so I could get to know you better."

She let out a quiet laugh. "And man, you sure got your money's worth, didn't you?"

The drive back to her apartment felt totally different than the drive to the restaurant had. I walked her to the door and said, "I'd like to do this again." She turned toward me without saying a word and enveloped me in the longest, strongest hug I'd ever enjoyed. We just stayed there at her front door hanging on to each other. When we finally stopped she kissed my cheek and said, "Call me."

Over the next few months our lunches and happy hours started to grow into a relationship. She'd agreed to share my interest in mountain biking if I indulged her passion for antique and consignment stores. Eventually we began sharing weekends at my house. The quiet, soft-spoken woman I'd first met had slowly become a talkative, fun loving companion. On a chilly Saturday in late November the threat of rain changed our plans from a ride in the hills south of town to a visit to a new antique store near her apartment.

The store had the by now familiar, musty smell of old wood, old fabric and old everything else. Maria usually wanted to head straight to the vintage jewelry cases first but we'd no sooner stepped inside when she turned to the right and walked toward the back corner of the store. I followed behind her and asked, "What are you looking for?"

A few steps later I looked ahead and got my answer. There, on a long, rustic wooden bench sat Uncle Rudy, Anna and Albert. I was shocked to say the least. I looked at Maria who just stood in silence in front of the trio. The store wasn't crowded and the quietness seemed appropriate. I stood a few feet back from the bench and waited. Maria took a step forward and stopped in front of Uncle Rudy for a moment then slowly moved on to Anna and Albert. I could see that her eyes were wet. She held her hand over her heart and with each stop she mouthed something I couldn't hear. After a very long, silent pause she turned to me and with her voice breaking, said, "I came to say goodbye to them."

A Visit to Tatum

As many times as I'd driven the stretch of I-44 between St. Louis and Springfield you'd think I would have figured out all of the best places to stop for a bite and exactly how much gas I needed to have in my tank. Over almost three years and a dozen trips I'd never had any problems until that day last month. Ordinarily if I'd left my house without a full tank I knew a stop in Cuba or Rolla would take care of things, but there was so much going on at the office I hadn't paid attention to details like that. Now, just past the Cuba exit my fuel warning light came on. It meant I'd be able to drive about twenty-five miles on what was left in the tank but it was thirty more miles to the Rolla exit. Should I risk the drive? It was farm country with no roads to use for an exit and U-turn back to Cuba. It seemed like I'd be forced to do a white knuckle drive with one eye on the road and one on the gas gauge. Then up ahead I saw a highway sign that I'd never paid much attention to on my previous trips. It read "*Tatum Exit 27*". I'd probably seen the sign before but it just didn't register in my memory. The warning light glowing on my dashboard told me not to take any chances. I hit my turn signal and eased my way on to the exit ramp.

At the end of the ramp was a small paved road that appeared to connect the exit and entrance ramps but not much more. There was no sign of a building let alone a town and I felt more than a little nervous. I had two choices, get back on the highway and hope I could make it to Rolla or turn on to the small road and see where it would lead me. Neither option was a good one but I chose to find out what was in this town of that I'd never heard of.

After about a hundred yards of driving through what felt like a tunnel of Pin Oak trees on both sides of the road I reached an opening. Off to my right was a faded, tattered sign that read *"Parker's Garage"* and under that *"Gas - Oil - Minor Repairs"*. A smaller sign below it that looked like an afterthought read *"Snack Bar"*. Up ahead on the left were three rows of identical mobile homes, all white and all in less than good condition. On the right past the sign was the entrance to a large parking area and a three-bay brick garage building. A small, white clapboard church sat at the far edge of the parking area. Beyond that, in every direction was a whole lot of nothing.

To call Tatum a town was a real stretch but all I needed was a full tank of gas and then I'd be on my way. There were no signs of people or activity as I slowly drove past a long row of mailboxes at the entrance driveway to the trailers. Each box had the owner's trailer address and name stenciled on it. There was a Parker, two Oldachs, three Larimores, two more Parkers, another Larimore another Parker and two more Oldachs. It was hard to miss the strangeness of all those trailers being home to just three extended families.

The two fuel pumps were near the garage and I pulled up to the one marked "Regular". There was no one in sight and after waiting for a few minutes I got out and grabbed hold of the nozzle. The readout showed I'd only pumped a quarter's worth of gas when I heard a man calling to me. "Whoa, hold on there, mister. That's my job!"

I turned and saw a skinny, middle-aged man in blue coveralls and a stained gray cap walking toward me. The name patch sewn on to his uniform read "Leonard". "Oh, sorry, Leonard," I said, "I thought it was self-serve."

The man took the pump from my hand. "Well, it ain't, we do the work around here." His total lack of warmth and even a hint of a smile were surprising.

"I guess a lot of people make that mistake, huh?" Trying to put a friendlier tone on the conversation didn't seem to have any effect.

"Nope, we don't get a lot of people here. Don't want to, cause we've got all them trucks to gas up and take care of." He motioned toward the far end of the dirt and gravel parking area where three identical red vans were parked on a patch of asphalt. From the striping on the pavement it looked like the empty spaces were for other vans that were elsewhere at the moment. On the side of each of them was painted "*Parker Delivery*". "That's why we have these pumps. They're for them trucks and the school van to Cuba, not for strangers."

"Then why the sign on the road over there? It makes it sound like you're a regular business."

That sign's nearly forty years old. Old Tatum Parker put it up back when he got his friends at the capital to put in the exit from the highway. He wanted the business and town to be somethin' the rest of us folks didn't."

The readout on the pump now showed that Leonard had already put more than enough into my tank to get me to Springfield so I wasn't reluctant to challenge him a little. "So then why didn't you just tell me that it's your gas only and send me on my way?"

"Wouldn't be Christian." He rubbed the cuff of his sleeve across his nose.

As he finished filling my tank I looked back again to the row of mailboxes along the road. I thought again how odd it was that all those trailers housed the members of only three families. Maybe it was wrong to pry but it was too late, my curiosity had gotten the best of me. "So, Leonard, I saw the names on the mailboxes and I don't see any other roads around here. Is that everyone in Tatum?"

He pulled the nozzle from my filler and looked at me. It wasn't a friendly look. "Yeah, that's Tatum; them trailers, the church and this garage."

"And are you a Parker?"

"Nope, an Oldach. Is that important to you?"

His demeanor was starting to piss me off but it was also bringing out my snarky side. "No, I was just curious. I've driven by this exit dozens of times and never noticed the sign for Tatum."

"That's the way we like it, nice and private." he answered. He pulled a rag from his back pocket, wiped his nose and said, "That's twenty-one seventy and we prefer cash."

"No problem, but I'll need a receipt from you."

Leonard let out a long, deep sigh and muttered, "Ain't that the way? There's always somethin' more."

I nodded and said, "Yeah, I guess there is." As I followed him to the garage I looked at the red vans again. "So what does *Parker Delivery* deliver?"

Leonard was not a patient man. He let out another deep sigh and answered, "You sure do ask a lot of questions. We deliver whatever the folks in Cuba and Rolla ask us to." It was a vague answer and I knew it would be the only one I'd get. We went into the garage and I laid two twenty dollar bills on the counter in front of him and then looked around.

The small area in front of the cash counter was barely big enough to stand in. The walls were covered with a large array of black and white photographs. They were portraits of what a banner sign on the wall said were three generations of the men and women who'd operated *Parker's Garage* and *Parker Delivery* over the years. That was the moment that I understood the mailboxes. There was Jim Parker and his wife Mary Oldach Parker. Next to them were Peter Larimore and his wife Cheryl Parker Larimore. Finishing the top row were Thomas Oldach and Margie Larimore Oldach and finally Nathan Parker and his wife Sandra Oldach Parker. I scanned the entire wall and every single face was attached to one of those three names. That explained the mailboxes and I figured it also explained Leonard's comment about wanting privacy.

It looked like Leonard was having some difficulty making change in the register and writing out my receipt. I let him struggle and looked into what the sign called a snack bar. There was a short red laminate counter with four stools and holes in the floor where two other stools had been removed. In front of that was a larger, empty area that looked like it might have been a dining room at some time in the past. I could hear noise from the kitchen but saw no one. I turned back to Leonard and asked, "Is there someone in the snack bar that can get me a coffee to go?"

He looked up from his mathematical struggles, appearing to be irritated by my interruption and said, "I suppose she can get you a coffee if you have your own cup."

"A paper cup would be just fine with me."

"Look, mister…what's your name by the way? I need it for the receipt."

"It's Wesley Ames."

"Okay, Mr. Ames, it's like I said before, we don't get a lot of strangers here. The men who drive them vans all live here and them boys like their coffee in a real cup." He went back to working on the receipt.

I shook my head, totally taken aback by his attitude. I walked out to my car and took out the insulated cup that I always kept filled with water. I poured it out on to the ground and walked back inside, right past Leonard and into the snack bar. A woman in the kitchen noticed me through the pass-through window behind the counter. She looked surprised to see a strange face. I held up my empty cup and called out "Coffee?"

She hesitated so long that I thought she was deliberately avoiding me. Finally she made it around the corner to the kitchen door and stood behind the counter. She said nothing and just stared at me.

"I was wondering if you could fill this with coffee for me. Leonard said you would."

"Leonard don't run the snack bar but I guess I can do it." She reached for my cup, looked at it a moment and said, "This is a pretty big cup, I'm gonna have to charge you extra."

"I sighed, not at all surprised that she was just as unfriendly as Leonard. "That's fine."

I watched her fill my cup and wondered how long that coffee pot had been sitting on a burner in an empty snack bar. She put the lid back on the cup, handed it to me and said in a monotone voice, "Three bucks even."

"Okay, I'll just give it to Leonard from my change."

"You weren't listenin' to me. Leonard don't run the snack bar. You gotta pay me."

I put the cup on the counter, pulled three singles from my wallet and handed it to her."

She took the bills from my hand and stood there looking at me. Finally, she said, "I accept tips."

I was really tempted to reach into my pocket and take out a dime but I just shook my head and handed her another buck. She took it without saying anything and walked back into the kitchen.

Leonard had finally solved the riddle of making change and writing it down. He handed me my receipt and change and without saying "Thank you" or "Have a nice day" like every other service attendant in America would do. He turned and walked away, into a small storage room behind the counter and closed the door.

The rest of my drive to Springfield would have been more pleasant if it weren't for my cup of bitter, boiled coffee and the bad mood I was in from my contact with the strange town of Tatum. A town like none I'd ever seen with people I'd hoped I'd never run into again. And they'd shown me very clearly that they felt the same way.

Before I'd left Springfield the next morning I'd made sure to top off my gas tank. One of life's lessons learned the hard way. My drive of two hundred and twenty one miles would be non-stop and, hopefully, uneventful. I wasn't surprised that right about the time I saw the exit for Rolla I started thinking about my strange experience of the day before. A town that I'd never heard of before was now all I could think about. I kept an eye on my odometer so I'd be ready in time to see the northbound sign for Exit 27 to Tatum and give it the finger as I passed by it. I slowed down a little when I got close to the area where I thought it would be. After a minute or so I spotted something ahead as odd as Tatum itself. A short remnant of the green metal post that had held the exit sign protruded above the grass along the shoulder. Someone, and I guessed it was Leonard, had cut down the sign. I looked across the median and saw that the sign along the southbound lanes was also gone. I pulled on to the shoulder and stopped.

A picture started to form in my mind. A picture of a skinny man in blue coveralls and a stained gray cap, holding a flashlight and a hacksaw. He was crouched in the darkness with the guardrails hiding most of him from view. Between passing cars he stood there and sawed away at the posts, first the northbound and then the south. I pictured his smile as each sign crashed to the ground and how he must have enjoyed dragging them into the weeds. And I pictured how his smile must have grown when he was sure that he'd just made it a lot harder for any strangers to find Tatum in the future.

I smiled, lifted my coffee cup and tipped it in the direction of Tatum. "Here's to you, Leonard Oldach, you strange man, and to your whole strange town." I took a sip of my coffee and added, "And on behalf of every single driver who will pass this way, I swear if you hadn't cut them down I would have."

Counterfeit

Some people would say Alex was in a rut but he preferred to think of the start to his day as his morning Zen. A double latte with skim milk along with one warm cinnamon roll, enjoyed outside on the pier at the table in front of the slip where he moored his boat. The pier was quiet at that time of day; a few charter fishing boats heading out to beat the midday rush of tourists and a handful of people opening the small shops and cafes that sat shoulder to shoulder along each side of the landside entrance. After nearly four years in business as a charter captain and the owner of the best little bait and tackle shop around, the pier still had the idyllic, tropical flavor that the locals took for granted but that he'd learned to love. When you grew up in chilly Wisconsin like he had, the warm Florida sun and gulf breezes never got tiresome.

He opened his laptop and began his usual slow, one-handed entrance into his workday; scrolling through his files with his right hand and sipping latte with the left. His days working in an office cubicle were long behind him, Thirty-eight years old and he was living the dream. Naples was about the same size city as the one he grew up in but even though it lacked some of the things that Miami and other big cities had it was perfect for him. His needs were simple. And its proximity to Marco Island and Ten Thousand Lakes made it a perfect launching point for Fishbone Charters. The business had gotten off to a slow start but he'd grown it enough in three years to buy the bait and tackle shop at the end of the pier.

It was when he tilted his head back to take the final sip of his latte when Alex looked over the top of his sunglasses and saw him leaning on the wooden railing. Or thought he saw him. About fifty feet away a tall, slender man in jeans, a yellow tee shirt and a tan baseball cap was looking back at him with a faint smile. He had a beard and his long hair stuck out in every direction from under his cap. Alex put down his cup and stared at the man. He knew it had to be a coincidence, a stranger who just happened to look like Jack. What else could it be? Jack had died over a year ago when he'd fallen overboard in a sudden squall. Three days of searching had led to nothing; no body, no clues and no explanation.

Alex lowered his sunglasses and continued staring. The man's smile broadened. He stood up from the railing and began walking slowly, almost nervously toward Alex. The closer he got the more confused Alex became. When the man reached the table he cleared his throat and said, "I was pretty sure you'd be here. Old habits die hard."

Alex sat speechless as he looked up at the man.

"Mind if I sit down?"

After a moment Alex nodded and said, "Yeah, sure."

There was a long stretch of silence as each man waited for the other to speak. Finally, Alex managed to blurt out, "What the hell, man."

"Yeah, I know this is really weird. I've been looking forward to this day and dreading it at the same time."

Alex studied his friend's bearded face and rumpled appearance. "What happened to you? Where the hell have you been for the past year?" He crushed his empty coffee cup in his hand, his anger obvious.

"It's a long story. First I want to say how sorry I am. I was in a jam and couldn't find my way out so I just sort of disappeared."

Alex didn't even try to hide his feelings. "A jam, you were in a jam. What the hell kind of jam makes you pretend to be dead?"

Jack's smile was gone. "Hey, man, I know you're pissed at me right now but just give me a few minutes and I'll explain."

"You disappear, put me through hell, hurt the business and you can explain it all in a few minutes. This should be good."

"Look, I know my being gone has probably been hard for you."

"Hard? Do you want to know what hard is? Hard is standing in front of a church giving a eulogy for a friend who everyone thought was taken too soon. Hard is trying to keep a business alive after one of the partners is dead. I even had to deal with some guy from the government calling me about you and asking how and where you died. Does all that sound like it was hard?"

"Wait, what about the guy from the government, who was he? What did he want to know?"

Alex was surprised that, out of the entire conversation, Jack had chosen that particular comment to ask about. "It was some guy from the Treasury Department. His name was, uh, Hackett, Paul Hackett, and he wouldn't say much except that he wanted to know about your activities. Not just your part of Fishbone, but also like the stuff you did at your graphics job and the times when you worked at home. He even wanted to know if you had any other friends who might be able to help him. It was all kind of mysterious."

"So what did you tell him?"

Alex sighed and leaned back in his chair. "Look, man, we have a hell of a lot to talk about and I'm just not in the right mood to do it now. I need some time to absorb all of this." He gathered up his cup and paper plate from the table and stood up. "I have a four hour charter to Cape Romano this afternoon. How about meeting me on the boat later, around five?"

"Jack stood up and looked around. "Can we wait until eight or so, after it's dark out?"

It was a strange request but Alex shook his head and muttered, "Yeah, okay, but make sure you show up"

Jack hesitated and then extended his hand to Alex. Alex just looked at him, his arms at his sides, and said, "See you around eight."

For the entire day it was almost impossible for Alex to think about anything but the sudden reappearance of his friend. It was as though he'd had a conversation with a ghost. For the past year he'd forced himself to accept that Jack was gone and that Fishbone had gone back to being a one man operation, and a struggling one at that. Now he wondered if he'd be continuing on his solo path or bringing Jack back into his business and his life. Despite Jack's once in a while financial investments Fishbone had always been a one man show with Alex as the partner who actually showed up and worked every day. They'd hired Melanie, an attractive and hard working young woman to run the bait and tackle shop but Alex still had to spend time overseeing the operation.

The afternoon charter ran a little longer than planned but Alex still had time to get home to shower and grab dinner. As he drove back to the pier he'd wished he had a way to reach Jack so he could cancel their meeting. There was too much emotion in the air; relief that his friend was okay and anger that the same friend had treated him that way. He'd sat in a chair on the starboard casting deck of Fishbone for half an hour when Jack finally showed up. He was wearing the same clothes that he had on when they met that morning. There was a faraway look in his eyes that Alex had never seen before.

Jack stood on the pier for a moment looking back over his shoulder and then left and right before he swung a leg over the gunwale and stepped aboard. He was carrying a small cooler and set it on the deck by his feet. "I brought beer in case you didn't have any on board."

Alex feigned gratitude. "Thanks," was all he said.

Jack looked around at the boat. "Looks like you've been putting some hard miles on Fishbone."

"Yeah, it's gotten kind of rough. Without your monthly contributions I've had to put off some maintenance. It's not easy going it alone." He'd hoped that Jack got that message.

Jack knelt down, opened the cooler and popped the top of a can. He slid the cooler closer to Alex as if the beer was some kind of peace offering. The tension in the air was as thick as the humidity. Jack sat down in a chair on the port side opposite Alex and, again, looked back over his shoulder. Finally, Alex asked, "Okay, let's hear it. Where in the hell did you disappear to and, more importantly, why?"

Jack took a long, deep breath. "Man, I've thought about this moment for a year and I had every word worked out but now…"

"How about starting with the why before we get to the how?"

"Fair enough. The whole thing started almost two years ago. I had a project at the office and the graphics had to be way beyond a Photoshop kind of thing, something so detailed that I had to create my own software upgrade. It turned out to be pretty cool and I decided to have it copyrighted."

"Well, good for you but you still haven't told me the why."

"Alright, I'm getting to that. So after using it on a few projects I got an email from a guy I never heard of. His name was Sam Rubio. I never did find out how he heard about me. He said he wanted to talk to me about a project that he had in mind and wanted me do it as a moonlight job. He said I shouldn't talk about it to anyone. And his message ended with "This could be extremely lucrative for both of us." So of course that got my attention."

Alex reached down and took a beer from the cooler. "Keep going."

"So, I met with Rubio and when he told me what he wanted me to do I almost pissed my pants." He paused, looked around and then looked right into Alex's eyes. "The guy wanted me to make counterfeit money for him."

Alex blew out a long breath. "You've got to be kidding. I hope you turned him down."

"Now I wish to hell I would have but he made it all sound so easy and profitable and he said he'd be taking all the risks. I confess that I bought his whole spiel and agreed to do it."

"So, just like that, you became Jack the counterfeiter."

"Hey, lower the volume, you know how voices carry over water. Anyway, through the whole thing I looked at Rubio as the counterfeiter and I was just the artist. He sourced the special paper and the inks and other supplies. I scanned the real bills and my software and his printer did the rest. It was all pretty cool.

Alex couldn't believe what his friend was saying. "So whatever made you think you could be in this line of work?"

"Oh hell, I was doing fake IDs way back in high school and it was how I got my spending money in college."

"There's a hell of a difference between helping a guy buy beer and making fake money."

"I know, and I never even thought of doing something like this until Rubio found me. He was the guy in charge, the teacher. He was the one who told me most counterfeit bills were twenties and larger so a guy could make a lot of money fast. But he wanted to just do fives and tens because the stores and banks didn't check them as carefully. He said they just took them from the customer and put them in their cash drawer. He said the risk would be next to none and he'd be the guy peddling the stuff I made. It would take longer to make the money but the safety would be worth it"

Alex leaned back, looked up at the stars and said, "Un freaking believable." He took a minute to drain his beer then looked at Jack. "So what did you do with all of the money you made?"

He grinned. "Do you mean the money I made or the money I earned?" It sounded like a snarky response even though he hadn't meant it to be.

"I mean your part of the take, your profits."

"Well, I banked some of it. Rubio made direct deposits to my account every month. That was how I could help you pay for the new downriggers."

Alex's eyes widened. "You mean those were bought with illegal money?" What the hell were you thinking? Now I'm somehow part of all this."

"Look, it seemed okay at the time. I only did it for about six months and then I told Rubio I needed a break. He wasn't happy but I was firm with him. And we never got caught."

Alex sat there looking down at the deck and shaking his head. "So it's over then, you're done with it all?"

"Yep, I guess so. Back to the real world."

"And your magic counterfeiting software, what about that?"

Jack got a more serious look. "I'm not sure yet. Rubio wanted to buy it but I decided to hang on to it, at least for now."

"You still haven't told me about where you've been and why you just disappeared like that."

It took Jack a long time to reply. He stalled, fished around for another beer and took a few sips. Finally he said, "This is the hard part." Another long pause then he said, "That day on the boat, the day I went over the side. It was all planned. I had a mask and air tank hanging over the side from a cleat. When the weather got crappy and we started bouncing around you were at the wheel and the two fishermen went down below. I was glad they were so nervous because they didn't even look my way. I grabbed the mask and tank and slipped over the side. There are so many little islands around here that it was easy to reach one underwater."

"That takes care of the how but I'm still waiting for the why."

"Okay, here it is. Remember I told you we never got caught? Well I guess Mr. Rubio was being watched by some guy so he told me to keep out of sight. I made myself some new ID and I'm going by my middle name now. I haven't heard anything from Rubio so I don't know how it turned out with that guy who was watching him."

Was it the Treasury guy who called me asking about you?

"Yeah, I think it probably was the same guy. What did you tell him?"

Alex shook his head. "Do you have any idea what it's like being on the other end of questions like, "How much do you know about your friend's financial situation?" and "Would your friend have any reason to hide from the law?" I had no freaking clue what to say to him."

"Look man, I'm sorry I put you through all that stuff. I never thought things would go that way."

Alex sat in silence. He was overwhelmed with what Jack had shared with him and he wasn't in the mood to hear any more. He used his foot to push the cooler back to Jack. "That's all, man. I have some thinking to do."

Jack understood. He'd been surprised that Alex didn't come totally unhinged. Before he picked up the cooler he took his phone from his pocket. "Do you still have the same number?"

Alex nodded, "Yeah, same one."

Jack punched in the number and hit Send. "There, now you have mine. Call me if you want to. I've been staying at the Best Western Naples Plaza. I've been doing some freelance work for a company in Miami so I'll be heading back there tomorrow."

"Why Miami?"

"It's bigger, more places to hide."

Once again they'd parted without a handshake or any kind of friendly words for each other. Alex wasn't sure if they were current or former friends and that bothered him as much as the things Jack had done. The busy season for both the shop and the charters was starting to wind down. There was more time for maintenance and more time for Alex to think about Jack's predicament, and whether it was also his predicament. He wondered how a nice down to earth guy with all of that talent could dig himself such a deep hole.

A month later the winter tourist season began to fade and the demand for fishing charters was low enough that Alex could consider taking some time away from the boat to travel somewhere. He hadn't been home for a family visit in over a year. A friend in Colorado had invited him up to the mountains for some late season skiing. He'd even wondered if he should ask Melanie out and spend some time getting to know her on a more personal level. Lots of options but his concerns for Jack stood in the way of making decisions about anything. He knew he had to say or do something

After a two week break without a charter reservation Alex was glad when he got a call for a two-man excursion to the Cape Romano area. It would be a leisurely afternoon of island hopping while things around the pier would be relatively quiet. It gave him an idea.

Alex was standing on the foredeck when he saw Jack, beer cooler in hand, walking toward the slip. He thought how it felt like old times and hoped it would turn out to be at least something close to that. Jack stepped over the gunwale, waved toward Alex and called, "Permission to come aboard?"

Alex smiled. "Same old smartass, I see."

They each went about the duties of getting the boat ready to go and joking with each other. It almost felt like the past year had never happened. Jack was stowing things down below when Alex saw a car pull up to the gangway. "That must be them," he called down. Jack came up on deck while Alex went to the wheel and started the motor. Two men got out of the car, gathered their fishing gear from the trunk and climbed on board. Jack showed them where to hook up their poles and stash their belongings while he unhooked the mooring lines. Then he signaled to Alex and the boat slowly pulled away from the pier and out into open water.

Jack stood waiting for the men to finish and then stepped forward with his hand extended. "Welcome aboard, I'm Jack Maines and that's Alex Walker up there at the wheel."

A tall man with thinning hair shook Jack's hand. He nodded toward his friend. "That's Bill Kovacks and I'm Paul, Paul Hackett."

Hiding in the Family Tree

It had been about three years since I'd tried what thousands of other curious people had; I'd bought a home DNA kit and traced my family's history. It was just an effort to satisfy my curiosity and find out more about my roots than I'd been told growing up. A couple of my friends tried it and said it was an amazing experience to learn details of ancestors they never even knew existed. My own experience included a very big surprise. My report went back four generations, to Ireland and America, and the maps and family tree diagram filled in so many blanks for me. It was a very complete picture of the Ryan and Clancy families with one exception. My great-grandfather on my mother's side didn't appear to be the great-grandfather shown on the family tree. His DNA didn't appear in my grandmother. Another DNA profile showed up in hers along with my aunts and uncles, my mother and me. The test explained it with the disclaimer "Due to often incomplete birth and health records of past generations there is a margin of error to be expected on some results." My DNA report was labeled "Inconclusive". I'd written it off to a technology glitch and hadn't thought much about the test again until that Monday in June.

Sitting at my kitchen counter after getting home from work, I'd sifted through the daily mail like always. Mixed in with the bills and junk mail was an envelope from the law firm of Murphy Kelly and Simon. It was addressed to Mr. Sean Thomas Clancy, very formal. Mail from a lawyer tends to get your attention so I pushed everything else aside and opened it. It was as short and to the point as any correspondence I'd ever received. It read, "Dear Mr. Clancy, our firm would like to meet with you to discuss an inheritance matter that we believe will be of great interest to you. The unusual nature of the inheritance and its source would best be dealt with in a personal meeting rather than via mail." The rest of the letter was instructions for who I was to contact to arrange a meeting at their office. I read it over a second time. What it said wasn't nearly as intriguing as what it didn't say. There hadn't been a death in the extended family for a decade so it seemed like some kind of mistake. But an inheritance, even a mysterious one, isn't something a person ignores.

There's a certain kind of pretentiousness to lawyers' offices and Murphy Kelly and Simon's digs didn't disappoint. The receptionist greeted me and led me to a large, impressive conference room. I was standing at the window looking out over the outskirts of Alexandria to the Capitol beyond when a tall, slender man walked in. "Hello, Mr. Clancy, I'm Carl Luther. Thank you for coming in. As I said in my letter we feel this matter is best dealt with face to face,'"

We shook hands and I replied, "That's fine. My office is only a few blocks away. Besides, that word inheritance definitely gets a person's attention."

We'd just sat down at a beautiful, mahogany table when a man walked in. Luther introduced him and said he'd been assigned to tracking the inheritance and its eventual payout for a number of years. The man, Paul Ratcliffe, spread some paperwork on the table in front of him and then looked at me. "Mr. Clancy, before I begin the details of this matter, let me start by saying that in all of my years of practicing law I have never been involved in anything quite like this. I'm the sixth lawyer in this firm to work on it going back nearly a hundred years. It began in our Dublin, Ireland office before our London office took over. Then about thirty years ago it moved here to the DC office. In essence, our firm has followed this case and your family around for four generations and now we're here to finally take it out of the file, dust it off and make it active."

For the next twenty minutes Ratcliffe carefully told the story of a man named Patrick J. O'Brien from Dublin. I didn't recall seeing the name O'Brien anywhere in the Ancestry DNA findings. Apparently, Patrick O'Brien had been the secret lover of Mary Ryan, my maternal great-grandmother. Their tryst resulted in my grandmother, Martha Ryan. There was no clear indication that my great-grandfather knew of his daughter's true lineage and from all accounts it was large, happy family. So there it was; an illicit love affair in my family. I wasn't sure what that meant to me so I just let Ratcliffe continue.

Patrick O'Brien was a self-made man. He'd grown up poor and spent much of his youth on the shabby backstreets of Dublin. He'd learned to live by his wits and handle whatever came his way. What often came his way were illegal transactions of all kinds; selling stolen goods, laundering money and doing questionable favors for city politicians. By the time he was in his late twenties he'd amassed what in those days was a small fortune. As he got older his fortune got bigger. He'd become a major player in the Irish Mafia and a prominent resident of Dublin. But it was when he was thirty that he'd met and fallen in love with my great-grandmother, a good Catholic woman, a married woman. There was no record of what had happened in the years after that other than the fact O'Brien had continued his criminal enterprise and that my great-grandmother had given birth to six children.

Ratcliffe stopped and looked at me. "I know that's a lot to take in so I'll stop for a moment."

I nodded. "Yeah, it sure is. So there was this gangster, this Patrick O'Brien, who had a fling with my great-grandmother. That was ages ago. What does that have to do with an inheritance for me?

Ratcliffe looked over at Luther and smiled faintly. "Well, Mr. Clancy, Sean, this is the part of the story that brought our firm into this matter all those years ago. Do you have any questions at this point?"

"Nope, but I have to say so far none of this was anything close to what I expected."

Ratcliffe's smile broadened. "Then wait until you hear this part." I leaned back, crossed my arms and let the lawyer continue his story of the Irish criminal who'd been part of my family, sort of. Apparently when my great-grandmother had told O'Brien of her pregnancy he begged her to leave her husband and make a life with him. It no doubt would have been a comfortable life but my great-grandmother being the good Catholic that she was turned him down. Out of his love and respect for her he agreed to keep the situation a secret just between the two of them. But when she bore a son, John Patrick Ryan, it led O'Brien to hatch a very unusual scheme. He couldn't share his wealth with his biological son so he decided to share it with a descendant of the boy, a child that would not be born for many years, far enough into the future when he could honor his love for Mary Ryan and there would be no way to connect the two of them.

Ratcliffe paused a moment to separate three sheets of paper from the stack in front of him. Luther looked at me like he was searching for my reaction to what I'd heard to that point. I felt like I owed him something. "Okay," I said, "it looks like you're getting closer to me."

Ratcliffe nodded. "Exactly." He looked over the three sheets of paper and held them up. "Mr. Clancy, this is why we asked you here today."

He paused a moment then got back to the story of Patrick O'Brien. Even though the man had known his fortune had come from illicit sources he saw it as fair compensation for his years on the streets. Sadly, since he couldn't share it with Mary Ryan he brought his idea to the office of John Murphy, the founder of their law firm. He sat down with Murphy and unspooled his lengthy and complicated scheme. He wanted to bequeath his fortune to the tenth-born male descended directly from Mary Ryan, upon that man's turning thirty years of age. Without admitting it to Murphy he knew that would be long enough to protect her name and reputation. Knowing it could take decades he structured a deal with the lawyer to compensate them for an ongoing effort to track the family. His estate was more than large enough to pay for their services for many years.

When Ratcliffe mentioned the tenth-born male in the family I closed my eyes and tried to picture the family tree that I'd gotten from the DNA study. I tried to remember every name hanging from every branch. Ratcliffe interrupted my thoughts. "Sean Thomas

Clancy, you are that tenth-born male descendant of Mary Ryan and Patrick O'Brien."

I looked at Ratcliffe then at Luther, shaking my head. "Holy cow, this is so bizarre."

Luther leaned toward me and said, "Sean, before you get too far in your elation there's a part of the story that we have to finish. I hope you're ready for it."

I looked at Luther and asked, "What do you mean? What's left to tell?

Ratcliffe took a deep breath and said, "Sean, there is a condition attached to the inheritance, a condition that must be met before any moneys are transferred to you."

Having been told about what an odd and eccentric man O'Brien had been it didn't exactly surprise me that there might be strings attached. I sat up straight in my chair and said, "Okay, let's have it."

I could see the uneasiness on Ratcliffe's face. "Sean," he said, "as I explained to you, Patrick O'Brien was a product of the streets. He took a strange pride in that. Everything he'd accomplished, everything he'd acquired came from his living by his wits and his courage." He looked over at Luther a moment then turned back to me and said, "Sean, there's no way to sugarcoat this. For you to inherit O'Brien's estate, which as of this morning's market reports is worth over one hundred eighteen million dollars, you'll have to live on the streets for exactly thirty days."

I hadn't thought of anything but the inheritance for two days; who it came from, the amount and mostly why I'd been chosen. I'd also realized it was a good thing that I was an only child. But nothing like the conditions for inheritance had ever entered my mind. I sat there almost numb.

Ratcliffe slid a two page document across the table to me. "Look that over while I explain the ground rules. "You'll be required to live without a fixed domain of any kind and find your own shelter. You'll be relocated to a portion of the City of Alexandria sufficient in distance from your current home so that you cannot easily find aid or assistance from a familiar person. You will start the thirty days with your wallet that may contain nothing but one form of identification and the sum of fifty dollars. You may not carry a credit card or any other instrument of commerce. You'll have no cellphone."

I had trouble reading the agreement document they'd given me while I listened to his chilling list of conditions so I stopped.

Ratcliffe continued. "You will wear work-type pants and a long sleeve shirt, a light jacket and a cap. You may carry one small bag or satchel that will contain just one change of clothing, one bar of soap and three pieces of fruit. Additionally, you may carry a pocket knife with a blade no longer than three and a half inches." He paused and said, "Sean, if you're wondering, that's an exact list of what Patrick O'Brien had when he started living on the streets."

Luther chimed in, "And Sean, this is important, you'll wear a GPS monitor so you can be tracked. There will be a signaling switch on the monitor to contact us should you decide not to finish."

I'd never imagined experiencing anything like what the condition document required. My comfortable and predictable life would be turned upside down. That is, if I agreed to do it. "What happens if I say no?"

"Then the entire estate goes into a charitable trust in Ireland which our office there will administer."

That night I struggled with the fact I'd agreed to the deal, without knowing if I could get through it. My lifestyle was comfortable and predictable. I couldn't remember a time in my life when I was truly hungry or without the security of friends and family. That would all change when I stepped out of the lawyer's car at my unknown destination. I went into my office the next morning and told everyone I had to tend to a family emergency, which in hindsight wasn't too far off the truth. Fortunately I had a pretty good sized backlog of vacation time. I was sort of between relationships so I didn't have any romantic entanglements that would complicate things. Two days later a driver picked me up and drove me to a run-down area south of the downtown. It felt like a foreign country to me; empty buildings, boarded up storefronts and streets devoid of traffic. It even smelled different. As I stood at the curb holding a knapsack that held the only the allowable possessions that would help me survive, I watched the car drive off. The conditions for the inheritance had officially begun and I was already frightened about what laid ahead.

I'd walked through the neighborhood for most of Day One trying to get a read on things. Were there other homeless people around? Were there any operating businesses that might be useful to me? Was there a safe place to sleep at night? Fortunately it was June and the nights wouldn't get too cold but I'd still have to face rain and wind. I slept that first night on a park bench using my knapsack as a pillow and a piece of cardboard as a blanket. At times that same cardboard served as a mattress. The first few days taught me how far fifty dollars could take a person. Even eating only convenience store take-out food burned through much of my money. On Day Four I knew I'd have to start panhandling.

I'd encountered some other street people who'd just looked in my direction then turned away. One afternoon, from a block away I'd stood and observed an encampment of makeshift tents, and large cardboard boxes that housed about a dozen people. Piles of people's belongings were interspersed with those who were lucky enough to have grabbed a shopping cart to hold theirs'. .I'd decided for my own safety it would be best to keep my distance. But on Day Five I met an elderly man, Walter Nowacki. I knew his name because he wore a name badge from a previous job pinned to his ragged coat. Walter took the time to give me advice on how to make it through each day. He'd been homeless for nearly two years but somehow still managed to smile. He gave me advice on how to keep the boredom from driving me crazy. He even laughed when he told me what to say when I approached someone for a handout. My first attempt was in front of a supermarket. I slowly approached a woman loading her car but even using my friendliest approach brought nothing, not even recognition that I was standing there. That was something Walter told me to prepare for, the being ignored. He said, "Sean, better get used to being invisible." I learned that the nasty looks and cold-hearted comments were nothing compared to being made to feel that you didn't exist.

By Day Ten my approach had gotten good enough to bring in around ten dollars a day in change and dollar bills. It was also the day when I'd realized I didn't smell too good. Paper towels and the sink in a gas station restroom became a daily ritual. It was also how I cleaned my teeth until one day when I used some of my food money to buy toothpaste and a toothbrush. Day Fifteen, the halfway point in my ordeal, or maybe I should say challenge, brought me to the decision to change into my other set of clothes. That was the day I'd learned that it costs as much to wash clothes in a laundromat as it does to eat a meal at McDonalds. The decision to look clean or fill my stomach was an ongoing problem. Carrying shaving materials was not an allowable part of the conditions and buying it all could mean I didn't eat for a day or two so my beard looked worse every day. It was a struggle to maintain any sense of pride when I saw my reflection in a storefront window and especially when I saw daily evidence of Walter's advice, when I was invisible to the people around me.

I'd crossed paths with Walter a few times and each encounter with the kind old man was gratifying. But on Day Twenty-three that changed. I found him curled up on a piece of cardboard in an alley by a warehouse. He was unconscious. It took me ten minutes to flag down a police car but they reached him too late. I'd never felt such loss. It had been just over three weeks since I'd become homeless. My situation was temporary but it was still almost unbearable when I woke up each morning and wondered what threats or challenges the day would bring. I couldn't imagine how Walter had lasted as long as he had, along with the other people out there with nowhere to go.

On Day Thirty the clock on the Marine Bank sign read ten-thirty three PM when a car pulled up to the curb. The passenger window went down and the driver called out, "Mr. Clancy, you've met the terms of the agreement." I got into the car and we rode silently back to my house. I slept for twelve hours before I felt like showering and eating a hot meal. I spent the rest of that day and most of the next thinking about, assessing and measuring my thirty years of life.

I sat at that big conference table a few days later, feeling better and looking cleaner. I'd decided to keep the beard and had spent quite some time learning how to trim it. I made small talk with Carl Luther, mostly about the facts of life on the street. Despite the fact I had met the challenge of the conditions the conversation felt strangely uncomfortable and I wanted to stop talking about all of those things I'd hoped I could forget. I was glad when Paul Ratcliffe walked in and changed the subject.

"Hello, Sean, welcome back to the real world." We shook hands and he sat down opposite me. The mix of emotions I'd felt was hard to describe; everything between mental exhaustion and total elation. There was the usual exchange of pleasantries and then he slid some paperwork across the table to me. Resting on top of the stack was a cashier's check for the sum of one hundred eighteen million, forty-one thousand six hundred and eight dollars.

I couldn't say anything or do anything except stare at that check. For thirty days I'd been thinking like a pauper, a vagrant just to stay alive and at the same time thinking of what I'd do as a wealthy man. I looked at both Luther and Ratcliffe and said, "You know, this check was the only thing that kept me going this past month, thinking about how I'd spend it but now that I have it…well, I don't feel the way I thought I would."

Ratcliffe replied, "I'm sure you're a bit overwhelmed right now."

"Yeah, I really am. Overwhelmed doesn't begin to describe it. I have all this money and all I can think about are the people I've encountered while I was going through this. Starving people. Sick people. People doing things they never imagined they'd have to do just to make it through one more day. The invisible people." I stopped a moment and thought about Walter and everything he'd dealt with, and the other people drifting along day by day. I leaned forward, holding the check and asked Ratcliffe, "Can you guys help me figure out a way to put most of this into some kind of charitable trust like Patrick O'Brien had in mind?"

Both men smiled. Ratcliffe answered, Sean, I think Mr. O'Brien would have been proud to call you his family."

Conversation Starter

Maybe it was from watching too many episodes of CSI on television or all of the crime and detective movies he'd seen, but the crime scene that Aaron had walked through that Monday morning was disappointing. There was no dead body, no signs of a struggle and no missing cash. The only indications that a crime had been committed at all was the rear door that had been pried open and kicked in and a safe in the office, its door also pried open. It had only been two months since he'd passed his detective exam. It was the reason he'd joined the police force and he was eager to dig into a big, juicy mystery of some kind. This wasn't it. When the phone call had come in from the bakery owner the shift lieutenant forwarded it to Aaron with the comment, "Sorry, man, it doesn't look like what you were hoping for."

The owner of the bakery, Warren Franks, had called to say there'd been a break-in and he thought something was missing. He didn't say what it was. When Aaron stood in the tiny office in the rear corner of the kitchen, looking around to assess the situation, he couldn't decide if a crime had really been committed. The safe was an inexpensive, office supply store grade built into the wall, its door still hanging open and exposing the interior. Aaron put on latex gloves and carefully looked over the contents. Neatly arranged on the left side was some miscellaneous paperwork held together with a binder clip, a strand of art glass beads in a wooden box and a small stack of bills, mostly fifties and hundreds with a thick rubber band around them. To the right of the items was a large empty space.

He stepped back out into the warmth of the kitchen. Franks stood near a large oven. Two women clad in white stood quietly on the opposite side of the room. Aaron wasn't sure how to start the conversation except to state the obvious. He looked at the man and asked, "Mr. Franks, was that stack of currency in the safe before the robbery or did you put in there afterward?"

Before answering Franks looked at the women and said, "Okay, let's get these ovens filled up, we open in two hours." While they began pulling trays from the cooler Franks turned his attention back to Aaron. "First of all that's not our safe, I mean it's not the bakery's safe. It belongs to my Aunt Sadie, Sadie Hart. She started the bakery back in the eighties and she's pretty much retired now. I run the place. That office is sort of her private space. Nobody goes in there but her."

"So you don't know what she kept in the safe?"

"No, not really, it's all her stuff. When I got here at six o'clock I saw the door had been broken in. Her office door was open which was strange because usually she only comes in at night after we're closed. I walked in and saw the safe hanging open. When I saw the empty space in it I figured whatever had been there was what the thief was after."

Franks' response did nothing to answer the big question. Aaron paused to choose his words carefully. "So... whatever it was, it was... somehow more important than a pile of cash. A pile of cash sitting no more than six inches away from it."

Franks seemed to be as confused as Aaron was. "Yeah, I guess. It seems strange to me too but that's Sadie's little world in there and I don't know much about what goes on in it. I'm not sure what else to say."

Aaron's first case wasn't proceeding the way he'd hoped it would and it didn't seem that Warren Franks would be of much help in solving it. The logical place to turn next was a conversation with Sadie Hart. Franks wrote down her phone number and address and after Aaron had taken a series of photographs of the back door, office and safe he got into his car and headed for her house. He knew he had to check in with his lieutenant to give him a progress report but it would be a report with a big hole in the middle of it so he decided to wait until after he'd spoken with Sadie. It took him awhile to find her house. It was a small bungalow-style cottage set back in a dense grove of trees that made it hard to see from the road. It was almost hidden from view.He stood by his car and looked around for a moment before he walked up the sidewalk and rang the doorbell.

A few moments later a slender, barefoot woman with long gray hair, wearing blue jeans and a flowered blouse slowly opened the door, but only wide enough to see him. "Can I help you?" she asked warily.

"Uh, yes, ma'am, I'm Corporal Hastings from the Santa Clara police department. I'm investigating a break-in at your bakery." He handed her his business card through the narrow opening, looking for her reaction.

She hesitated before opening the door wider. She was clearly shocked. "When? What happened?"

"Well, Miss, or is it Mrs. Hart?"

"It's Ms. Hart, I'm divorced."

"Okay, Ms. Hart, sometime last night someone pried open the backdoor of the bakery and entered the kitchen. They also went into your office and pried open the safe. I spoke with your nephew, Warren, and he told me that you were the only one who ever used the office. I'd like to ask you a few questions if you don't mind."

Her shocked look remained and she seemed unsteady on her feet. "Yes, please come in." She led him into the living room and said, "Please sit down right there." She motioned toward an ornate armchair upholstered in bright, geometric fabric and then sat down cross legged on a wicker peacock chair. Aaron looked around the room. The scene was like something right out of a 1970s movie.

Aaron waited to see if she wanted to speak first but when she just sat there staring at him he decided to start. "Ms. Hart, when I spoke to your nephew he told me that the office is yours and yours only. He said he never goes into it so he had no idea what the thief might have been after. The cash in the safe was never touched and neither was the necklace. But whatever was on the other side of the safe is gone."

Sadie looked down at the floor then at Aaron. She asked, almost as if she was pleading, "Can you find who did it? Can you get my... my stuff back?"

"Well of course we'll do whatever we can but right now the problem is we don't know what we're looking for. That's why I came to see you. Can you fill in the blanks for me?"

She looked visibly uncomfortable and didn't say anything right away. Finally, she asked, "Do you like sourdough bread?"

Any thought that he was getting closer to an answer evaporated with her question. "Well, sure I do. Who doesn't?"

"We make all kinds of baked goods but sourdough is our signature product. It was all I sold when I first opened."

Aaron still had no idea where she was going with her story. "Okay, so you make sourdough. What's that got to do with the break-in and the safe?"

Their conversation seemed to be making her increasingly uncomfortable. "Look, Corporal, this robbery has me kind of rattled. Can we talk later, maybe tomorrow?"

Aaron tried to be polite and hide his frustration. He couldn't tell if she was truly upset or just trying to hide something. "I know this is a shock for you and I understand, but I seem to be investigating a theft that right now just looks like a second rate breaking and entering."

She stood up, a signal that she didn't want to talk anymore. He let out a long sigh, stood up and said, "Ms. Hart, we really want to help you and your nephew with this case and it's going to mean that we meet again to talk about it. I need to know more."

She looked down at the floor. "I'm really sorry, Corporal, I really am. Just give me until tomorrow, okay?"

Aaron realized there was nothing else he could do so he replied, "Okay, I'll call you tomorrow. You have my card if you'd like to talk sooner." She was still standing in the doorway as he backed out and drove away.

He called his lieutenant on the way back to the station. It wasn't a conversation he wanted to have. He'd spent a good part of the morning investigating something he couldn't understand and trying to explain it made the whole thing sound even stranger. Since there was no clear definition of what had been stolen and no one had been hurt the lieutenant told Aaron to write it up as an in-process investigation and move on to another case that had just been called in. All Aaron could do was to follow orders but he couldn't stop thinking about the bakery. He decided he'd work on both cases at the same time.

He sat at his desk the following morning thinking about the many things he'd learned in his detective schooling and from conversations with veteran cops. The one overriding piece of his training that stuck with him was that you couldn't understand the crime unless you understood the people involved in it. He'd been unable to shake the feeling that Sadie Hart was holding back something she didn't want to talk about. It was time to learn more about her.

He started with her birth records at the courthouse. Having her complete name and birth date gave him a start for a Google search that told him she had graduated from the University of California at Berkley with a degree in Analytical Chemistry. It was an odd background for someone in the bakery business. That was where his search had gone cold. He knew if he was going to find out the whole story he'd have to talk to people who knew Sadie personally. After a side trip to investigate a store burglary downtown he drove to the bakery to talk with Warren Franks. He waited for a few minutes while Franks finished up with a customer then followed him back into the kitchen. Twenty minutes of conversation gave him some interesting information about Sadie. Franks also went on a tangent and gave him the history of sourdough bread all the way back to the California gold rush. When Sadie had first opened the bakery she'd built a large following of customers looking for the classic sourdough flavor. Franks had walked Aaron through the baking process with an emphasis on the starter dough. He told Aaron about how the original fermented dough he used was created by Sadie back in 1996 and refreshed with additional water and different types of flour periodically ever since. That starter was the basis of the bread he baked every morning. She had been keeping a record of it in a small, spiral notebook and had shared parts of it with him. When Aaron asked him what was the secret of her starter recipe he replied that sourdough bakers are competitive and never reveal their secrets.

The last few minutes of their discussion focused on Sadie herself. After college she worked for a small chemical lab in San Francisco and got married. Her husband had urged her to stay at home and have children but Sadie was a free spirit and the marriage hadn't lasted long. She moved to Santa Clara, lived alone and bought and ran the bakery until she'd sold it to Franks in 2014. Since then she'd stayed out of the day to day operations but sometimes came in at night after the bakery closed to work on baking her own special breads.

After their meeting Aaron stood outside on the sidewalk looking over his notes. It didn't seem as though he'd made much progress. He'd learned more about making sourdough than he had about Sadie. He'd just turned to walk to his car when a voice behind him called, "Excuse me, sir, can I talk to you?" A well dressed man approached him and asked, "Are you the police detective that's been helping Warren with his break-in?

"Yes I am. I'm Corporal Hastings."

"I'm Bob Montini. I own the jewelry store across the street there and I live in the apartment above it. Warren told me about the break-in and I was wondering if he told you about the after-hours stuff."

"No, what do you mean after hours?"

"I mean when Sadie goes into the bakery at night alone."

"Yeah, Warren told me she likes to go in to keep her hand in the dough business so to speak."

"Yes, that might be the case but I think there's more to it than that. Whenever she's in there working, a car pulls up out front and waits."

"Waits for what?"

"For Sadie. They wait awhile then the outside light blinks and she comes to the front door. The driver gets out and they talk, then he hands her something and she hands him a white box, a bakery box. Then she goes back in and the guy drives away."

Aaron thought for a moment then asked, "How often does that happen?"

"Oh, about twice a week, sometimes more. I've even seen cars with out-of-state license plates. When Warren told me about the break-in I immediately wondered if it was one of those people in those cars."

The man's story was surprising and it posed more questions than answers. Aaron thanked him for the information and walked to his car. It seemed like the time was right for another conversation with Sadie Hart, mystery baker. He'd thought about calling her on the way to her house but the idea of a surprise visit appealed to him. He was thinking like a detective.

He'd rung her doorbell twice and just when he'd figured she wasn't home he heard the latch and saw the doorknob turning. Like his first visit Sadie only opened the door slightly. When she saw it was him she opened it the rest of the way. He noticed the same uneasy expression on her face. "Good morning, Corporal," she said softly.

"Good morning, Ms. Hart, do you have a few minutes to talk now?"

She sighed and nodded. "Come on in, and I think it's okay for you to start calling me Sadie."

They went in and sat in the same chairs in the same 1970s surroundings as they had the day before. She sat nervously while Aaron took out a small notepad. He hesitated then reached into his sport coat pocket and took out a small black device. "Sadie, would you mind if I recorded our conversation?"

She was silent for a moment then replied, "I'd prefer that you didn't. Let's just talk."

Recording a victim interview was standard procedure but without her permission he backed off. "Okay, let's talk. How about telling me about what goes on when you work in the bakery alone at night."

The color drained from Sadie's face and from her expression it was clear that she wasn't expecting that question. "What did Warren tell you?"

"He just said you liked to go in at night once in a while and bake your own breads which I can totally understand. And he told me about the history of sourdough and wow, he's really into it. But it's what your neighbor across from the bakery, Mr. Montini, told me that has me puzzled. What about all of the cars that pull up out front and the people you meet at the door with a white bakery box?" He stopped. It was Sadie's turn to talk.

She still looked nervous but she took a deep breath and began her reply. "Okay, yesterday you asked what was taken from my safe. It was a starter, a sourdough starter to make a few loaves." She looked at Aaron and saw the curious expression on his face. "Wait, I have an idea for how I can explain this. I'll be right back." She got up and walked into the kitchen. A few minutes later she returned and handed him a small, warm loaf of sourdough. "Here taste this while I explain things."

Aaron broke off a bite sized piece and put it in his mouth. Sadie watched him for a moment, as if looking for a reaction, and then continued her explanation. "As Warren probably told you the sourdough business is very competitive. Every baker tries to come up with the perfect recipe and the perfect flavor. Each starter recipe has its own chemistry. I keep mine in here."

She handed him a worn spiral notebook and waited while he broke off another piece of bread, put it in his mouth and then started to read her notes. After he'd looked at a few pages he said, "Holy cow, this is like a foreign language. It looks pretty technical for just a bread recipe."

She smiled. "Like I said, it's chemistry. My background is in chemistry and over the years I found ways to, well, let's just say use various ingredients and chemistry to enhance the flavor. The starter that was in the safe was my newest recipe."

Aaron was feeling mellow and relaxed as they talked. He'd already eaten nearly half the loaf and broke off another piece before he asked, "So do you think whoever stole the starter could figure out the recipe from it?"

"No, all they might get is what I did in the basic leavening process but I hadn't finished the final refreshments yet, my enhancements. So the fermenting still had a long ways to go."

"So it looks like that was what somebody wanted bad enough to break in and steal, somebody who had tasted your bread before. It's not much to go on but at least now I have a lead." He leaned back in his chair, totally relaxed and staring at the ceiling. There was a strange, satisfied smile on his face. "Sadie, what do you call this bread I'm eating? Is it just regular sourdough? Man, it's so good I don't want to stop."

Sadie had a smirk on her face. "That's one of my customers' favorites. I call it Miner's Delight."

"Well it sure has me feeling delighted," he said, almost slurring his words. "Can I buy a loaf?"

Her smirk turned into a smile. "Sure, but I'll need a few days. Stop by the bakery on Friday night, make it around eleven. Stay in your car until I blink the light by the front door. I'll meet you there. This one will be free but when you come back for more please pay in cash."

Limelight

In these days of technology and reality TV can we really be certain of what we're seeing, of what is real and what isn't? Modern life happens at a frenetic pace. We have lots of time to see and hear things but no time to absorb their meaning. Before we can comprehend what we just experienced we move on to the next one. That was the inspiration for an idea of mine, something I'd been working on in my mind for a long time.

That Saturday when I'd looked at the clock and saw it was almost four o'clock I thought, "Holy crap, a whole afternoon come and gone." I was known to criticize people who spent hour after hour on social media and here I'd been doing the same thing. Besides sending half a dozen tweets I'd perused *Instagram, Tik Tok, Tumblr* and even *Facebook*. One would think that a person who works in media all week long would find a different way to relax on weekends. Ordinarily I'd feel guilty about it but this time was different. This was recreational and I knew the idea swirling around in my head could quite possibly lead to a lot of fun. I'd been waiting for Matt and Amy and when they arrived I planned to let them in on my little con.

Four o'clock on a Saturday afternoon seemed like an appropriate time for a beer even though noon was my acceptable starting time on weekends. I'd no sooner popped open a can when they knocked on the door. Matt held the door open while Amy carried a cardboard box through and handed it to me. "Just some more miscellaneous stuff before we make the final move," and then she kissed me. After months of discussion we'd agreed it was time for her to move in with me and my small house was filling up with her things. Organizing it all was a work in progress.

As I'd expected Matt had his laptop with him. Like most computer geeks he never went anywhere without it. He laid it on the coffee table and asked, "Alan, is it self-service today or are you going to get me a beer?"

"You can get it yourself. Just follow the path you've worn into the floor for the last two years."

When Matt had his beer and Amy had her wine we sat down around the coffee table. "Okay," I began, "You're probably curious about my wanting to get together today." They both nodded. "We've all been working hard lately and it just seemed to me that we need a little escape, an adventure that I think will be a lot of fun." They sat there looking at me, waiting for me to get to the point." "Okay, picture this. We pool all of our talents and technical skills and create an identity, a person. To be specific a Country music star who'll only exist online."

Matt looked curious but sounded skeptical. "That's been done before. Lots of people have fake emails and *Facebook* pages. How would this be any different?"

Amy added, "Yeah, there are all kinds of fake people and bots on the internet."

I fully expected their responses. "The difference is we'll be giving birth to the complete package, a guy who'll look absolutely real, sound real, with photos and videos of himself and he'll even correspond with his fans."

Matt again showed that he was the skeptic of the bunch. "So this guy hasn't been created yet and he already has fans. How does that work?"

"Well, his first fans will be fakes because we'll have to create them. I'm thinking Twitter accounts and probably Facebook too. But little by little he'll get noticed and followed and liked by real people on every website we decide to put him on."

Again the skeptic spoke up. "You said videos. How do you make a video of a guy who doesn't exist?"

Amy set her glass down and said, "I was wondering the same thing."

Before I said more I handed each of them three printed pages, an outline of what I'd named *Project Limelight*. I gave them a moment to scan the pages and then launched my explanation. "This scheme will involve all kinds of media to make it work. We'll need photos, video, text and, of course, music."

Amy was intently reading the outline. "I see you included creating a website for the guy and you have that task here under my name."

"Yep, you're the one who's done that and knows exactly what's involved in creating and managing it. Everything else we do with the guy will revolve around his website."

I was waiting for Matt's skepticism to turn into enthusiasm but he was still tentative. "I see you have getting the guy's photos under your name and mine and that's not a hard thing to do. But let's get back to the video part. That's under my name so how about filling me in."

It was hard for me to control my enthusiasm. "That's key, and one of the most interesting parts. The TV stuff you did for the car dealership last month fit into my marketing plan perfectly. That's the kind of thing we'll need for this project."

"Geez, that wasn't much of a technical challenge, just putting a man and woman's heads on each other's bodies and sticking them into a convertible. How does that tie into your scheme?"

It was clear that the conversation was getting into details so we all grabbed another drink and opened our laptops. I sent them the file for *Project Limelight* and we started in on the plan.

It began with an introduction to our new singing sensation. I pulled a photo from my Pictures file and sent it to them. "Okay, guys, meet Buck Henson. He's thirty-two, from Dalton, Georgia and he's been playing in clubs for about three years. He's being called a traditionalist with a contemporary sound and he's working on his first studio album."

Amy leaned toward me. "Okay, you said we're creating a fake guy but that's a real guy there. Who is he?"

"His name is, or was, Joe Dudley. He was an obscure solo artist in the 1980s and died in 1991. He never really made it big but I like his voice. It took me awhile but I found a couple of videos of him on *You Tube* that only had a couple of comments attached so he's not remembered much."

"And why him?" she wondered.

"Well, to be blunt because he was good and now he's dead."

Amy's eyes widened. "Oh my God, I can't believe you said that."

Matt chimed in, "Yeah, that's pretty cold, man."

I realized I should have used softer phrasing. "I didn't mean it to sound so harsh it's just that if we do this we can't use video that links to someone who's still performing. I checked and Joe Dudley never married so he didn't leave any offspring. He's pretty much been forgotten."

Matt returned to his original line of questioning. "So you have video of this guy and you mentioned my commercial. Again, how does all this tie together?"

Amy looked just as uncertain as Matt did and I knew I owed them some details. "Like I said one of the keys to this will be the video part. You've probably heard the term "deep fakes", where you record like a half hour or more of video of a person's face and head from every direction and the person using every kind of facial expression, You also record the person talking so when you put his head on the video of the other person's body you can make it look and sound like he's saying what the other person is. That part is tricky but when it's done right it's amazing."

I was surprised when Amy sat up straight and looked me in the eye. "Honey, that's really scary stuff. I know it's very new but I've read where people are already using it to embarrass politicians and even worse."

Matt added, "Yeah, that's some scary stuff. I've seen it. Let's be careful here."

"It's only scary when it's done to hurt someone or make money illegally. We aren't doing any of that. This is strictly for fun."

I could always count on my girlfriend to be the voice of reason. "Honey, I must admit this sounds interesting but I still don't see where it all leads. Why do you want to do this?"

It was time for me to try and close the deal. "Okay, let's all admit it. We work in and live with media and cyberspace and we see the crap that people find interesting. Even worse we see the crap that they believe. They follow the old saying that if it's on the internet it must be true. Haven't you ever wondered how far you could push that envelope?" I looked for some kind of reaction from them that would tell me if my pitch was working but I saw nothing. "Look, you guys, there's nothing in this plan that will hurt anyone. We're not going to ask for money or have any direct personal exchange with anyone. It's a harmless prank on a scale that no one's ever tried before. We'll be creating the newest up and coming music star but he won't really exist. Imagine the challenge of it all and how it will feel when we pull it off."

They both had slight smiles and I took that as a positive sign. They were silent for a moment and then Matt said, "Well I guess I'm in as long as there's nothing illegal or harmful. And I confess, I've been curious about the technology of deep fakes ever since I first heard about them."

Amy nodded and said, "Me too. I'll have to do it in the evenings but I'm in"

Before I could respond Matt said, "Alan, there's just one thing I want to know. Who's going to be the face of this Buck Henson?"

I grinned and said, "You're looking at him."

Amy looked at Matt for his reaction then said, "You've always had that rock star fantasy. I see it on your face every time you play your guitar." She turned back to Matt. "You should see him. When he's got his guitar in his hands it's like he's in a different world."

I felt like I needed to defend myself. "Every guy who ever picked up a guitar has had the same fantasy. Maybe this project is part of my fantasy but I promise you that's all it will be."

Monday morning brought a continual exchange of emails between the three of us. I could tell that after Amy and Matt had had time to absorb the concept of *Project Limelight* their enthusiasm had grown exponentially. On Sunday night Amy had used a template she'd developed for her employer, made some tweaks and created the framework of the Buck Henson website. Matt had spent the evening researching deep fakes and said he had come up with the basic approach he wanted to take with the *You Tube* videos. After a couple of hours I'd written a backstory of Buck's life and Googled the lyrics to the songs in the videos. And, what might have been the smallest but still a critical task, I'd found a fake beard online. It was a good match with my hair color and was full enough to mask my real identity. The mustache would hide enough of my mouth to make it easier for Matt when he attached my head to Joe Dudley for performance scenes. I'd lip sync the performance and was confident it would pass for the real thing.

The project quickly took on a life of its own. The three of us worked separately on it in the evenings and exchanged our results the next day. Amy came over and helped me fit the beard and mustache to my face. She did such a good job she kissed me and said, "Wow, I think I could fall for this Buck Henson guy." Matt and I had gotten together so he could take still photos and make the video of my head and of me singing the lyrics. When we met again at my house the following Saturday we had a lot to talk about. We put our laptops in front of us on the table. The excitement was palpable.

Amy looked like she was ready to burst. "Let me go first, you gotta see this!" The website came up on our screens and it looked great. An image of sheet music formed the banner at the top and a large picture of Buck was smiling out from the center. There were smaller still photos scattered around the second page. "This is where Matt's videos will go. I created fourteen fake names for *Twitter* accounts and I'll put comments from them on the third page which is what I call Fanbook. When real comments and photos start coming in they'll go there too."

I leaned over and kissed her. "Great work, babe. I can't believe you got that far in one week."

She smiled. "I have to confess the whole thing got me way more excited than I thought it would when we first talked about it."

"I feel the same way," Matt chimed in. "You have to see this first video." He brought it up on his screen, sent it to ours and a few moments later we watched and heard Buck singing to a live audience. "I have to touch up a few things but all in all it looks real, and you were right, Alan, the facial hair made it easier to do the lip sync. You notice that I modulated the sound so Joe's baritone voice turns into Alan's tenor."

"You mean Buck's tenor," I interrupted. "He's almost real."

"Yeah, you're right. And also, I created seven fake *Twitter* accounts."

It was my turn and it was hard to contain myself. "Here, I'm sending you a selfie video I did on my phone. It's an up close and personal comment to all my loyal fans. I'm telling them about the work I'm doing in the studio. You're going to love these song titles I came up with; *Is it Really You?*, *Love in Disguise*, *I Thought I Knew You* and my favorite one, *How Far Can We Go?* I also created eleven *Twitter* accounts.

Both Amy and Matt broke out in laughter. "Wow," Amy said, "great titles. Too bad nobody will get it but us."

We spent nearly two hours drinking wine and deciding on final details. In a few days *Operation Limelight* would be going live. After that the world would finally meet Buck Henson.

It's been said that on the Internet nothing lasts more than a week. We were glad to see that wasn't the case for our project. With all the fake *Twitter* names talking about Buck and the likes, comments and shares on multiple websites he had come to life. His *You Tube* videos garnered a ton of comments about his traditional sound, his genuine country style and even a few on his cute beard. We sat there for a few minutes scrolling through the site then Matt broke the silence. "Holy crap, this thing looks so real."

Amy was smiling. "Honey, you did it, you actually gave birth to a star! What's next?"

The buzz we felt wasn't from the wine, it was from doing what we'd set out to do and we agreed that we didn't want to stop there. Buck Henson was real or so thought a few hundred people on the internet. Those hundreds would soon be thousands. To keep things going Buck would do weekly interviews with updates on the album's progress and answer questions from his followers. I'd even come up with the title of the album: *Do You Believe Me?*

The interviews were hard at first. Matt handled the video and Amy played the part of an online music writer. She asked me questions that we'd spent hours preparing. The scripts included my answers to questions from fake fans. Mark D. from Phoenix wanted to know if I wrote my own songs. Rebecca M. from Norfolk asked if I'd send her an autographed photo and Lisa W. from Louisville wanted to know why I wasn't married. Those questions led to many more from real people. In a strange way, albeit an artificial one, my fantasy was coming true.

Two weeks later the online fan activity had grown to thousands but Amy and Matt's enthusiasm was fading. We all enjoyed the fact we'd accomplished an amazing goal but none of us knew what to do next. We'd been so caught up in the adventure of giving birth to Buck Henson that we hadn't taken time to realize it couldn't last forever. I couldn't deny the pleasure of being semi-famous but my partners seemed to be getting bored.

Matt and I were driving back to town on a windy afternoon after taking a set of still photos at his uncle's farm. There was one of Buck standing by a horse, several of him sitting on an old split-rail fence and a few of him sitting on a wooden bench playing guitar with his hair blowing in the wind. The photos would help keep Buck alive a little longer.

Matt's old car had been on the edge of collapse for a long time so I wasn't surprised when it died on the way home and we had to pull off the road. We were standing outside the car on the shoulder of the road waiting for the tow truck when a black BMW slowed down and pulled in front of us. Two young women got out and seemed nervous as they approached us. They stopped and the driver stared at me, turned to her friend and said, "See, I told you, it's him, it's Buck Henson!"

It was my first live fan encounter and I wasn't sure what my reaction should be. I smiled and said, "Yeah, it's me." I looked over at Matt and he had a strangely nervous look on his face. "My friend's car broke down and we're waiting for a tow."

The driver asked, "Well, while you're waiting would you mind if my friend took my picture with you?" She had a wide-eyed, star struck expression.

"Sure, I'd be glad to."

She moved beside me and clutched my arm. I felt my Stetson blowing off and clamped my hand over it. Then I felt it happen. My beard, my expensive, fake beard started to peel off in the wind just as her friend took the photo. "What the hell is this?" the friend shouted. The driver looked at me and quickly let go of my arm. "You have a fake beard? That's creepy, are you even a real person?" She looked over at Matt then back at me and said, "And if you really were a big star you wouldn't be riding around in that crappy old Toyota." She walked back to her friend and they looked at the photo on their phone, shaking their heads. The looks they gave me as they got back into their car made me realize my little world of internet stardom was beginning to unravel.

That evening Amy and I tracked the latest activity on the webpage, *Facebook* and *Instagram*. The women from the BMW were Michelle and Caitlyn. They'd posted the beard photo on both of their Twitter accounts and Buck's fan page. Their comments weren't exactly kind. "What a fake" and "Attention everyone, Buck Henson's a big phony." During the course of the evening the photo made the rounds of their friends' Instagram and Facebook accounts. By the time we went to bed it looked like our little media adventure had come to a screeching, embarrassing halt.

When I got home from work the next day it was clear we had to shut things down. The number of angry people was evidence that we couldn't keep it all together or talk our way out of things. We knew this day would come eventually but not like this. We had created a person, at least an electronic version of one. While it had been a fun little adventure it was tinged with a scary reality; the internet's power to sway gullible people was downright dangerous.

Matt joined us at my house and we opened a few beers then sadly went about working on our areas of responsibility. Amy took down the website and social media sites. Matt deleted the videos and I deleted every photo, file and bit of text that ever showed Buck Henson existed, except for one photo of Buck smiling and tipping his hat to what were now his former fans.

We sat silently for a while, each of us lost in thoughts of what we'd done and where it might have gone. We'd never come up with an endgame. Finally, Amy said, "Well, that's that. It was fun while it lasted."

I turned my laptop to face the three of us, Buck's face filling the screen. We hoisted our glasses toward him and Matt said somewhat sadly, "Rest in peace, Buck Henson."

There were a few silent minutes and I knew I needed to break the dour mood. I wasn't sure if it was the right time to mention it but I couldn't resist. *Project Limelight* had been an interesting experiment. Working around the edges of fact and fiction had become addictive and I wasn't ready to put it all behind me. I reached into my laptop bag and pulled out some paperwork. I handed them each three printed pages, an outline for my next project. "Okay, that adventure may be over but I have a new idea that you'll really like." They looked at me in disbelief but said nothing. I leaned forward and said, "Okay, remember that ten million dollar lottery ticket that went unclaimed last year and they couldn't find the guy who bought it? Well, picture this."

Navigator

"Geez, Charlie, when I told you to find us a car I meant something that would get us there and back not a piece of crap like this. Where'd you find it?"

"I got it at the Circle K. The guy left it running when he went into the store and I was standing right there and I figured it was easier than trying to hot-wire another car. I'm not so good with wires. I was scared shitless but I just jumped in and beat it out of there fast."

"Geez, this thing looks like it's older than you but I guess we're stuck with it." He looked directly at Charlie. "This job needs to go like clockwork or Manny will never give me more work. Without the money I make on this job there's no way I can get my car out of hawk. The bank made it clear they want every nickel of my outstanding payments or I'll never get the pink slip back."

"Sid, I know this is an important job. I need the money too so I can get a car of my own and take some classes at the community college. If we're just going to Chula Vista and back we should be okay. This car may not be new but it'll make it, you'll see."

"Well, at this point I guess we have no choice. I told your dad before he died that I'd look after you and teach you to make your way somehow. All I know is moving money around so that's all I can teach you."

They got into the car and sat for a moment to figure out a plan for the trip. They talked about the best route from South San Diego to Chula Vista but it was pretty much a one-sided conversation. Sid had the experience and knew his way around. Charlie didn't. As Sid talked about the trip Charlie just looked at him and shrugged. Sid looked at his young accomplice. "Since this car is stolen we'll have to stay off of the I-5. That's where all the cops will be and I'm sure it's on their hot sheet already. I think I can find us an alternate route to get us close but after that we'll be guessing our way. We have to find the pick-up location and then bring the bag back to Manny."

"Don't worry, Sid, I have a navigation app on my phone that we can use to get directions."

"Why does a guy without a car need a navigation app?"

"It's for when me and my friends are out. When there's a party or something going on we use it to find the place. And besides, it was free."

Sid rolled his eyes. "I have GPS on my car too but that doesn't do us any good today." He pulled a folded piece of paper from his wallet and handed it to Charlie. "Here's the pick-up address in Chula Vista. See if you can plug it into your app so we can get on the road."

Charlie sat quietly, first scrolling to the navigation app and then typing out the address. "Damn, it's not working," he grumbled and then tried it again. "I don't know what's wrong here, Sid, but when I put in the address the screen just sits there doing nothing then it shuts off." He tried it a third and fourth time with no luck. "Sid, my GPS is screwed up."

Sid looked at him with a surprised expression and immediately knew the problem. "Oh, man, I just remembered. I saw on the news last night there's some big time storm happening on the sun. It's like the biggest bunch of solar flares in years and they say it's going to mess up all the satellites for the whole day, maybe longer. Radio, TV, phones, the internet, everything's screwed."

"So that's why my GPS won't work?"

"Yeah, that's got to be the problem. Damn, and we have to find that house and get the money back here to Manny by tonight. I don't want to get sideways with him."

"What are we going to do, Sid? This is bad. We can't get him pissed off, especially when you're trying to teach me what to do."

Sid was silent for a moment as he looked around the car before he said, "Any guy who drives a shitty old car like this probably doesn't know about GPS. He's probably old school. Check in the glove compartment and see if there's a map. I'll look in the back."

Charlie came up empty but Sid found two roadmaps in a pouch behind the driver's seat. "Bingo, here's our Plan B." He got back into the front seat and handed one of the maps to Charlie. "Here, look this one over and see if Chula Vista is on it."

Charlie unfolded the map and looked it over. Sid could see the total confusion on the kid's face. "Something the matter?"

"Well, kind of. I never used a map before. I figured since I had GPS why the hell bother with a map. The computer woman tells you everything about how far you are away and where to turn and stuff."

"So you're saying when we head for Chula Vista and I ask you for directions off the map you won't know what to do?"

"Well I could probably figure it out if I had enough time."

Sid shook his head. "Time is a luxury we don't have." He took a deep breath and muttered, "Good Lord, people have outsourced their brains to gadgets."

Charlie was silent and clearly embarrassed.

"Okay, kid, you drive and I'll navigate. I'm going to show you how people managed to travel all over the place for years without a damn satellite or cellphone."

They switched places and sat for a moment while Sid studied the map. "Okay," he said, "Pull out here and make a left. We'll fill the tank at that Shell station over there then we're going to head up Smythe and look for the 905."

"How long will it take us?"

"I don't know exactly, probably about an hour and a half, two hours with traffic."

"My navigation app tells you exactly how long a trip will take."

"Look, Charlie, whether or not you realize it you're learning a little lesson here. When you rely on a machine, it owns you. You can't get along without it. Today you and I are in total control of things. Hang on, you just might learn something."

"Why didn't Manny give you directions?"

"Manny doesn't give directions, he gives orders."

After they'd filled the tank Charlie pulled on to the road and moved into the right lane. He was more than a little nervous. "Let's keep our eyes open for cops."

"Yeah, I know, but it will get safer once we're out of this part of town and headed north."

"So we're driving north?"

"Yeah, didn't you know Chula Vista is north?"

"No, I really haven't traveled much except for a trip to Phoenix to visit my aunt when I was ten."

Sid shook his head and sighed. "Okay, we're on Smythe now. We're going to stay on it and go under the 905. The name of the road will change to Picador Boulevard so watch for a sign."

"The name of the road changes?"

Another long sigh. "Yeah, they do that sometimes."

They drove under the 905 and Charlie excitedly called out, "There's the sign, we're on Picador!"

"Okay now, keep your eyes open. Stay on this road and when we get to Palm Avenue keep going straight through the intersection. The road name changes again to Beyer Way."

The drive had gone smoothly but as they approached Main Street they both saw the flashing lights of two police cruisers. "Shit," Sid growled, "looks like an accident and that's too many cops." He took a quick look at the map and said, "Quick, bear left up here and get on to Fourth Avenue."

Charlie swerved and the car went on to the shoulder of the road but he managed to maintain control. Sid looked out the back window and said, "Good, they're not moving." He looked back down at the map. "It's okay we're only a block off course. Stay on Fourth until we get to H Street then make a right." He looked over at Charlie and couldn't resist. "Your navigation lady couldn't have made that little adjustment for us."

When they got to H Street and turned Sid said, "Okay, we're getting close. In three blocks turn right on to First and then make a quick left on to Casitas Court and then stop. That's where the pick-up house is."

A few minutes later they were stopped and looking straight ahead at their destination. "What happens now, Sid?"

"What happens now is you stay here and keep your eyes open. If you see anything that looks wrong you turn around and get out fast."

"What do you mean wrong? Is this going to be dangerous? You never told me that."

"It's not supposed to be dangerous. Manny sets up everything and it always goes like clockwork but you have to be ready just in case."

Sid got out and slowly walked toward the small, unassuming house. When he got to the front door he turned and looked back at Charlie then rang the doorbell. Charlie was close enough to see a tall, stalky man with a goatee and a menacing look open the door. He was holding a black canvas bag. The two men spoke for about a minute but Charlie wasn't close enough to hear the conversation. Finally the man handed the bag to Sid then stood and watched him walk back toward the car before closing the door.

Sid came around to the driver's side and said, "Okay, Charlie, I'll drive us back." After they'd switched places Sid sat quietly for a moment clutching the steering wheel. Charlie could tell he was unnerved. "Something wrong, Sid?"

"No, it's just that big guy in the house. He's a different guy from the one I've been working with and he kind of creeps me out." He handed the bag to Charlie and said, "Put this on the floor between your feet where it's safe and then pick up the map and see if you can get us back."

Charlie's jaw dropped and his eyes widened. Sid grinned and said, "Just kidding."

They retraced their route, keeping a constant look out for police and being careful to maintain the speed limit. Charlie tried twice to see if his phone was back to working but had no luck. It was a quiet ride until Charlie asked, "So how long were you and my dad friends?"

Sid hesitated, thinking back over a lot of years and a lot of memories. "Well, I met your dad back in high school. We raised some hell in those days. After graduation we both got jobs at the aircraft plant and worked on the line together. On weekends we shot pool down at Dominick's and your dad ran the table on anybody dumb enough to challenge him."

"I miss him. He was always teaching me stuff and fooling around."

Sid looked over at him. "I miss him too, kid."

There was another long break in their conversation and then Charlie got curious again. "So I assume there's money in that bag?"

"Yep."

"How much?"

"I don't know. Manny never tells me."

"You said this morning all you know is moving money around. What did you mean?"

"Well, I'm part of a team, Manny's team. Each guy on the team has a specific job. Mine is to take the money and give it to Manny or someone else who takes it and gives it to another guy. That guy invests some of it and I take the rest of it to another guy. The money moves around enough and you can't trace where it came from."

"Isn't that called money laundering?"

"It's called my job."

They continued their drive south and about half an hour into it a police cruiser pulled into the traffic behind them. Sid saw it in the rear view mirror. "Shit, there's a cop two cars back." He slowly and carefully pulled into the parking lot of a strip mall and saw the cop continue on by. "I'll be glad when we're back to I can dump this junker."

. By late afternoon they'd made it to Imperial Beach. Charlie gawked in silence as they drove past rows of large, elegant homes and swaying palm trees lining the streets. When they turned on to Seacoast Drive he saw the oceanfront homes of what he thought must have been some very rich people.

Sid gestured toward a huge, white stucco mansion with a long, curving driveway. "That's Manny's place."

They pulled into the driveway and stopped in front of the arched portico. When Sid didn't try to get out of the car Charlie asked, "Aren't you going in?"

"You don't go to the door until you're summoned."

"How does he know we're here?"

"There are more than twenty cameras looking at the entire property and halfway down the block in both directions. Believe me, he knows when someone pulls up."

They sat for a few minutes and then saw the front door open. "That's my cue." Sid muttered. He grabbed the bag, got out and walked toward the house and under the portico. A casually dressed man with a mustache greeted him. "Sid, glad you made it okay."

"Hello, Manny, good to see you."

"What's with that piece of shit car? I pay you enough to drive something sweet."

"Oh, uh, I borrowed it while mine's being serviced."

"Who's that in the car with you?"

"That's the kid I told you about. I promised I'd help him out after his father died. He's the one who's looking for a job."

"I might be needing another driver soon. Can you vouch for him?"

"Yeah, no problem. His dad was a straight shooter and so is he."

Sid handed Manny the bag and waited while he took it inside. A few minutes later he returned with a large manila envelope. "Here you go, Sid. That's for today and I'll need you again next Tuesday. I need you to run up to National City for an exchange."

"Sounds good. I'll have my own car back by then. Just email me the address like always."

The two men shook hands and Sid walked back to the car. When he was back behind the wheel Charlie asked, "Did everything go okay?"

Sid nodded, "Yeah, everything's cool." He slid the envelope on to the seat under him and drove back out the driveway.

"Hey, while you were with Manny my phone started working again. Do you want me to plug in our route?"

"No, this is familiar ground for me, but thanks."

The ride back to Charlie's house was uneventful and quiet. Sid looked over at him. "Your mom's probably got your dinner ready by now. When Charlie didn't respond Sid asked, "Something bothering you?"

"Well, I was just thinking about the guy who owns this car. He looked like a nice enough guy and he's probably going nuts wondering where his wheels are. I feel bad for taking it even if it's a piece of junk. It's that man's junk."

Sid could tell that Charlie was bothered by his role in the day's activities. When they pulled up in front of Charlie's house it was starting to get dark. Before Sid could say anything Charlie asked, "What are you going to do with the car?"

"I'm going to drive it someplace a few blocks from my house, wipe it clean for fingerprints and leave the keys on the floor."

"Park it someplace where it'll be easy for the cops to find it so they can get it back to that guy."

Sid nodded and just sat looking at Charlie. Finally he said, "Kid, this is yours." He pulled the envelope out from under his legs and handed it to him.

Charlie took it and looked at Sid. "What's this? What are you doing?"

"It's your cut."

Charlie undid the clasp of the envelope and spread it open. "Holy shit, Sid, this is like a pile of fifties and hundreds!"

"I'm keeping the promise I made to your dad. This is my way of looking out for you. Go out and buy that car and take those classes."

"But what about a job working with you like we talked about?"

"This isn't any kind of future for a kid your age. Hell, it's no kind of future for a guy my age either. The money I move around is invested in all kinds of things and I'm investing my share in you."

Charlie stared at Sid, looked down at the money and then back at Sid. "I can't believe it. I don't know what to say."

"Don't say anything, just stay out of trouble. If I hear you screwed up there'll be hell to pay."

Charlie smiled. "Don't worry, my career as a car-thief is over."

As Charlie started to get out of the car Sid grabbed his arm and stopped him. Charlie, there's an old saying that goes, "If you don't know where you're going any road will take you there." He handed Charlie the map. "Hang on to this. You never know when your GPS might go out again. This official Sid Navigation System will help you find your way to wherever you're going."

Printed in the United States
by Baker & Taylor Publisher Services